WHAT THE HEX

ALSO BY ALEXIS DARIA

You Had Me at Hola

A Lot Like Adiós

Along Came Amor (coming soon)

Take the Lead

Dance with Me

Dance All Night: A Dance Off Holiday Novella

Amor Actually: A Holiday Romance Anthology

PRAISE FOR ALEXIS DARIA

Praise for What the Hex:

"A delightful read that is sure to enchant readers!"
    —Zoraida Córdova, award-winning author of *The Inheritance of Orquídea Divina*

"Sweet, sexy, and a little spooky, *What the Hex* by Alexis Daria is wicked fun. The amount of humor, hijinx, and heat packed into these pages is nothing short of magical."
    —Melonie Johnson, *USA Today* bestselling author

"A magical romance that reminds us real love gives the confidence to be our best selves."
    —Kari Cole, author of *Hunt the Moon*

Praise for *Take the Lead*:

"Believable, emotional, and hot—everything you want from a story about dance partners!"
    —Jasmine Guillory, *New York Times* bestselling author

"A sparkling debut...Daria's story of this behind-the-scenes romance is a perfect ten."
—*Entertainment Weekly*

"As irresistible and sexy as a Bad Bunny song."
—Adriana Herrera, *USA Today* bestselling author

Praise for *You Had Me at Hola*:

"A triumph of Latinx joy and feminist agency."
—*NPR*

"An absolutely pitch-perfect summer escape."
—*New York Times* Editor's Choice

"A multi-layered sexy, poignant, and fun story set against the glamorous and dramatic world of telenovelas. Filled with lovable characters, relatable family dynamics and the nuances of identity, Alexis Daria's novel is full of heart. Romance readers will fall head over heels!"
—Chanel Cleeton, *New York Times* bestselling author

Praise for *A Lot Like Adiós*:

"A charming, sexy spitfire of a novel! Between Mich and Gabe's crackling dialogue and their palpable yearning, I fell hard and fast for this book, racing through its pages until I finally closed it with an overflowing heart and a deep happy sigh. Romance readers, this is your new favorite book!"
—Emily Henry, *New York Times* bestselling author

"Second chance romance perfection! I was under this book's spell from start to finish, fanned myself several times (in the first hundred pages no less) and fell completely in love with Mich and Gabe. A TBR must have."

— Tessa Bailey, *New York Times* bestselling author

"Sizzling chemistry, realistic family dynamics, humorous fan-fiction flashbacks, and two strong leads make this outstanding second-chance romance one of the best yet by rising romance star Daria."

— *Booklist* starred review

WHAT THE HEX

A PARANORMAL ROM-COM NOVELLA

ALEXIS DARIA

What the Hex

Copyright © 2022 by Alexis Daria

Ebook ISBN: 9781641972376

KDP POD ISBN: 9798355354985

Along Came Amor Copyright © 2023 by Alexis Daria

Take the Lead Copyright © 2017, 2023 by Alexis Daria

Solstice Dream: A Summer Solstice Short Story Copyright © 2020 by Alexis Daria

Cover Illustration by María Dresden

NYLA Publishing

121 West 27th St., Suite 1201, New York, NY 10001

http://www.nyliterary.com

For all the brujitas who were told they were "too" anything.

You are magic!

CHARACTER LIST

Catalina "Cat" Cartagena
30 years old. Magical couture fashion designer. Enchantments, fabric alchemy, and telekinesis. Competitive and ambitious.

Diego Paz
Cat's high school nemesis-turned-love interest. 30 years old. Hot Miami chef. Food alchemy. Flirty and protective.

El Capitán
Immortal water spirit. Captains the Isla Bruja water taxi. Currently takes the form of an 18 year old boy.

Rosalinda Cartagena Vargas
Cat's mother. Exorcisms and necromancy. Hostess supreme.

Benito Cartagena
Cat's father. Financial and astrological advisor. Indulgent.

Carolyn "Caro" Cartagena
Cat's oldest sister. 31 years old. Sweet but passive aggressive.

Crystal Cartagena
Cat's younger sister. 28 years old. The funny one.

Cleo Cartagena
Cat's younger sister. 20 years old. Belle of the ball.

Corinne Cartagena
Cat's youngest sister. 18 years old. Mischievous.

Tío Nestor De León
Diego's great-uncle. Proprietor of the Crone's Nest Inn and collector of capes. Chatty.

Abuela
Cat's grandmother. Glamor magic and dance magic. Force of nature.

Matteo Paz
Diego's older brother. Gym rat.

Lorenzo Paz
Diego's younger brother. Jokester.

Josefina Paz De León
Diego's mother. High Moon Priestess of El Templo de la Luna. Haughty.

CHAPTER ONE

There's no place like home, right? Well, in my case, it's true. There's nowhere quite like Isla Bruja, home of rich witches, restless ghosts, and rampant chisme.

But with my older sister's wedding just three days away, even I can't make an excuse to get out of coming home. I am the maid of honor, after all.

Following a direct flight from New York to Miami, I take a taxi to one of the waterfront parks. There's a small wooden pier that goes ignored by the other parkgoers, but of course, I can see it. I drag my luggage to the end and reach into my purse for a coin. My fingers touch a piece of stiff, luxurious paper, and I pull out the wedding invitation instead.

Unable to help myself, I read it for the umpteenth time, hearing the words in my mother's voice.

You are cordially invited to the wedding of Carolyn Maria
Cristina Cartagena Vargas and Matteo Alejandro Paz De León,
hosted by Benito and Rosalinda Cartagena Vargas.
Join us under the light of la Luna to witness Caro and Matteo
joining together in magical matrimony.

This invitation admits the bearer plus one guest.

Across the bottom in bubbly script, my sister Caro scribbled,

Cat, for the love of Sol, bring a plus one!

I snort at the demand and shove the invite back into my purse. Who does my sister think she is? Even if I had a plus one, I wouldn't bring them, if only to show Caro she can't push me around. As second oldest, I long ago accepted my mission to keep her in check.

Even at her own wedding.

Rummaging in my bag, I eventually find a quarter and toss it off the end of the pier. It disappears before it hits the water. A moment later, a blue and white runabout boat with a small cabin appears, helmed by a slender young man with a deep tan and a flashing smile.

I blink at him in surprise. "Are you El Capitán?"

He whips the white and gold captain's hat off his head and bows in his seat. "At your service, mi sirenita. Call me Cap."

And then he pulls down his sunglasses and winks.

I resist the urge to scold an ancient water spirit for hitting on me and instead gesture at his appearance.

"What happened to your…self?"

The last time I visited my family and used the water spirit taxi, El Capitán took the form of a grizzled viejito who smelled like beer and grumbled in Spanish. Not an eighteen-year-old Casanova.

He shrugs. "Needed a change. Vamanos, muchacha."

Cap snaps his fingers and my luggage bounces jauntily into the boat. I take his hand and let him help me in. The seats are plush, and a small roof awning protects us from the glaring Florida sun. He touches the wheel, and a second later, we're off. Behind us, the pier shimmers, then disappears from sight.

The little boat leaves the shore and heads straight into the open waters of Biscayne Bay toward Isla Bruja, a crescent-shaped island that is both *there* and *not there*. It was founded in 1915 by a few magic-wielding Latino families from islands in the Caribbean —the Cartagenas and De Leóns from Puerto Rico, the Paz familia from the Dominican Republic, the Garcías from Cuba, and more.

Shrouded in magical mist, Isla Bruja is invisible to humans, and their boats pass right through. No one has ever successfully measured and mapped it, since the island changes shape and size according to the magical might of its residents.

Even though I was born there, I've been so disconnected over the last five years, part of me fears the island won't reveal itself to me. But I trust my driver.

Cap's boat cuts through the water easily, and after a few minutes of silence, he looks over his shoulder. I can see my reflection in the lenses of his sunglasses.

"¿Cómo estás, Catalina? Haven't seen you in a minute. Where you been?"

"Here and there. New York. Paris. Milan. London."

"World traveler!"

"Fashion Week never rests, and neither do designers."

"Still making dresses?"

Of course Cap knows about my former life as a designer of magical couture. Everyone on Isla Bruja knows everything about everyone else. El Capitán is technically the corporeal form of ancient elemental energies, but even he's up on the latest gossip.

The boat hits a wave and rears. Cap flips his middle finger at the water and yells, "La concha de tu madre!"

"Language, Cap," I chide playfully.

He shoots me a grin, and I'm grateful for the interruption. If I tell him that I ran off to New York because I got magical burnout, he'll repeat it to all of his customers until some other juicy tidbit captures his attention.

As the boat cruises through the mists obscuring Isla Bruja

from human view, the island takes shape before us, and I breathe a sigh of relief when I get a good look at my old home for the first time since my last visit nearly two years ago. Surprise surprise, the dock leading to my parents' property has expanded into a two-level affair with what looks like a full bar in the center.

Cap guides the boat alongside the lower level of the dock. Ropes shoot out and secure themselves to the mooring posts.

"Here we are, mi sirenita. Home sweet home."

Home, yes. Sweet is probably a stretch.

Before I can go inside, I must deliver the payment.

I close my eyes and touch my chest. It's been so long since I used my magic, it takes a moment to come. Finally, my fingertips tingle, and light appears around them. I gather the amorphous little ball of energy and pull it from within myself, holding it carefully in my fingers as if it's a sticky piece of cotton candy. I pass it to Cap, who takes it and pops it into his mouth. His eyes glow behind the sunglasses, and he nods.

"The trip is paid. Welcome back to Isla Bruja, Cat."

"Gracias, Capitán."

My bags lift into the air and bob merrily up the dock and toward the house's back patio.

I move to leave the boat, but Cap's arm shoots out lightning quick. A strong hand wraps around my wrist, and I stare at him in surprise.

He removes his shades and his eyes are the brightest blue-green, like tropical waters. His expression is serious, and he suddenly looks twenty years older. All traces of the flirty youth are gone. "Cuidado, Catalina Cartagena," he warns, his voice deeper than it was.

I nod. "I will."

It's been a while, but I know how to handle my family.

He releases me and I step onto the dock. When I turn to say goodbye, he and the boat have already disappeared. I turn and head up the stairs.

Welcome to Isla Bruja, indeed.

You'd think after being away for two years, one of my many family members could be bothered to greet me, but no. The land between the house and the water is empty and quiet.

Growing up, our home was a modest little mansion. Still big enough for my four sisters and I to each have our own rooms, but Caro and I shared a bathroom back then. I can't count how many times she passive-aggressively moved my blow dryer back over to my side of the sink whenever it dared to be more than a centimeter over her imaginary dividing line.

Now, Casa Cartagena is one of the grandest estates on the island. It's probably grown since the last time I visited. It's certainly bigger than it was when I started my enchanted fashion design business at the age of fifteen.

That business helped my family rise in power, and our house expanded of its own volition to match.

I stop and peer around. Is this even the right house? Sure, the dock is new, the pool is bigger, and there's...is that a tennis court? Oh, for the love of Tierra. None of us even play tennis!

And in my opinion, the Greek columns adorning the back door are a bit much, but I certainly won't be saying so within la Casita's hearing.

Otherwise, the basic structure and design are close to how I remember it. Clean white lines, arching windows, and a red tile roof. All surrounded by an overabundance of palm trees, of course.

But I don't see any signs of people, which is strange, considering there's going to be a wedding here in just three days.

I don't even hear music playing, or anyone yelling from inside.

There are wards around the house, but as a member of the Cartagena family, they can't keep me out. Still, when I reach the ward line, I feel a slight pressure on my skin, like walking through an invisible membrane.

My luggage is waiting for me at the back door. I open it and go inside. The air is blessedly cool after the humidity outside. Not even witches can control Florida weather. My bags follow me in.

"Up to my room," I tell them, and Cap's enchantment sends them on their way.

Now, where is everyone?

"Hello? Anyone ho— Whoa, what's with all the cameras?"

At least three people with shoulder-mounted video cameras swing my way, the dark lenses training on me like eyes. Eerily, the camera operators say nothing.

I raise an eyebrow. "Um, don't I need to sign a release form or something?"

"Cat? Honey, is that you?"

I turn at the sound of my mother's voice. She enters the room, preceded by the *click-click* of her signature stiletto heels. She's tall and stunning, with sleek black hair, golden brown skin, and dark eyes that hold all the secrets of death.

She is, after all, a necromancer.

I take after her, minus the death-eyes part. My powers lean more toward enchantments and alchemy. And much to Mom's chagrin, my wardrobe these days tends toward New York City black.

She totters over in a blood red bodycon dress, which, for her, is casual wear. She leans in to kiss my cheek and I catch the scent of her perfume, reminiscent of tropical flowers after a soaking rain.

"Hi, Mom."

"Cat, I'm so glad you're finally here. You're going to have to work double time to get enough footage."

I scrunch my face in confusion. "Footage for what?"

"The wedding video, of course!"

"Mom, don't you think this is overkill? There's what, three, four, *five* cameras? How many angles do you need?"

Mom laughs. "Oh honey, this is only the first-floor team. There are more cameras upstairs!"

"More? What are you filming, a documentary?"

"We just want to make sure every aspect of Caro's big day is recorded."

"But the wedding isn't for three more days. How long have the cameras been here?"

Mom's voice gets distracted and dreamy. "Hmm? You know what, I can't quite recall. Maybe your father will know. Benito!"

A roiling thunder cloud appears beside her. There's a loud crack and suddenly my father is there, with wisps of fog dissipating around him. He's wearing a blush pink guyabera shirt and white pants with leather sandals. His dark hair is slicked back and his moustache is perfectly groomed, as always. He slings an arm around my mother's waist and hugs her close.

"Sí, Rosalinda, mi amor? Oh Cat, you're back! How's New York been treating you?"

He releases Mom and moves in to hug me. He smells comfortingly of rum and incense.

"The label just finished another successful Fashion Week," I tell him. "I'm looking forward to unwinding while I'm here."

He pats my hair like he used to when I was a child. "Qué bueno, mija. That's good."

His narrow hazel eyes are usually sharp, but today they look a little unfocused. He hasn't quit patting my head, so I duck out from under his hand and stand next to Mom.

"Cat has a question to ask you, Benito," she says. "Cat, what was your question again? I can't remember."

She has the same dreamy look in her eyes. Is wedding stress getting to them? Are they on drugs?

"Uh, right, my question. How long have these cameras been here?" I ask.

Dad blinks. "Cameras? Oh! Uh...yes, the cameras *are* here. You'll need to record enough one on one interviews, okay?"

"Interviews? For a wedding video? What the hex is going on here?"

Mom winces. "Honey, don't curse on camera. It's gauche."

I sigh. That's my mom. Concerned about appearances, as usual. Time to change the subject. "Where's everyone else?"

Mom flashes a smile at the cameras before she answers. "Your sisters are in the ballroom."

"I'm going to go find them."

"See you later, honey. Don't forget about your interviews!"

"Sure thing, Mom!"

Yeah, right. I'm not doing any flipping interviews.

I wave goodbye to them and duck into a hallway that I hope will take me to the ballroom. With the way the house has changed, who knows what's popped up since I was last here.

I wander for fifteen minutes looking for the ballroom. My journey takes me through a tiled courtyard full of lush greenery that smells and sounds like a rainforest. Then I get lost for a while in an echoing stone corridor, where dust motes drift in shafts of light that come from nowhere. I also pass through multiple sitting rooms done in classic Miami style with clean white lines and the occasional pop of beige or blue.

In the last of these, something framed on the wall makes me pause.

Oh for… Who the hex put my high school diploma here?

I glare at it for a moment, then keep walking, but the memories aren't so easily left behind.

Like all the other young witches here, I graduated from Isla Bruja Preparatory Academy.

Unlike all the others, I graduated as salutatorian.

That's right. *Salut*atorian.

Second. Mothereffing. Place.

At the time, it felt like the worst moment of my life. Silly, right? But I'd been gunning *hard* for the valedictorian spot. Unfortunately, my rival, Diego Paz, had been jockeying for it just as fiercely. By the time we reached senior year, my fashion business was already booming. The night before a final exam, I stayed up late to finish a gown for Diego's mother, of all people. She's the current High Moon Priestess of El Templo de la Luna, and turning her down hadn't been an option, even though she'd been a nightmare to work with. I swear to Sol, this woman required so many adjustments to the design, it's a wonder there was anything left to the dress. Long story short, I didn't do as well on a divination test as I normally would have. That slight misstep gave Diego the edge he needed to take the top spot.

To this day, I wonder if his pendeja of a mother did it on purpose.

Bitter, who me?

I need to get over it, though. Diego's older brother is about to marry my sister, and the whole Paz family will be tied to mine forevermore. All because my creations made us famous. Before that, my dad was just a financial and astrological adviser to the richest families on Isla Bruja. Now, the Cartagenas *are* one of the richest families on Isla Bruja.

Hence this accursed corporate merger. I mean, wedding.

I finally find the ballroom and holy hex, it's four times the size it was when I was last here. It's decorated like something out of Versailles, which is fine if you're a dead French royal but kind of weird for a family of Puerto Rican witches. Round tables are positioned around the room, ready for the rehearsal dinner tonight and the reception on Sunday.

My older sister Caro stands between Matteo Paz, her husband-to-be, and our sister Crystal. Four camera operators loiter around them in a loose circle. Our two youngest sisters, Cleo and Corinne, are nowhere to be seen.

Caro's shorter than I am, but other than that, we could be twins. Same dark cat eyes, straight nose, pointed chin, and golden-brown skin. Crystal towers over both of us, and she has a big personality to match. Caro is sweet, but pushy. Crystal is funny, although her humor tends toward mean at times.

And me? I'm the ambitious one. The competitive one.

Caro's features are just a little more delicate and prettier than mine, and after years of having our faces compared and coming in second, I decided to differentiate myself by kicking ass in school. So what if I wasn't the pretty one or the funny one? I was the *smart* one. I excelled in all my classes, and my magic is more powerful than the two of them combined.

Was.

My magic...*was* more powerful.

Shit. Gotta remember that. It's easy not to think about it in New York, but here, everyone expects me to be like I was before.

Caro's fiancé is good-enough looking, if overly groomed for my tastes. Matteo's handsome features appear cast from bronze, cold and unyielding. His dark button-down and slacks are perfectly tailored to his bodybuilder physique, and so devoid of wrinkles, magic must be involved. His custom-made Italian leather loafers probably cost more than my yearly salary.

Lucky for me, I still have access to my family's money, if not their power. I work my ass off in New York because I want to, not because I need the money. If I can't be the best at enchanted fashion design, then damn it, I'll be the best with fabric.

I move further into the ballroom. Caro sees me first.

"Cat! You're here!" She pulls me in for a hug, and Crystal joins in. The scent of their perfume threatens to overwhelm me and I sniffle. Or maybe it's not the perfume, maybe it's just how much I've missed them. Caro's only a year older than I am, and Crystal is two years younger than me. When we were kids, we were the tightest group of brujitas you ever saw. Despite our differences, it's been hard to be away from them for so long. It's like missing a part of myself.

Caro waves me over to her fiancé. "Cat, come meet Matteo."

I wait for Crystal to point out that I've already met Matteo multiple times, that everyone knows everyone else on Isla Bruja. It's our dynamic, Crystal saying the blunt things Caro and I are thinking but would never say aloud. But when I look at Crys, she's just got a wide, sappy grin on her face, like she's never been happier than she is at this very moment.

I narrow my eyes. This is entirely unlike Crystal, who is, according to our grandmother, una malcriada. Aka, she's *never* happy.

The cameras move in as I approach Matteo.

He reaches out a hand to shake mine. "Nice to meet you, Catalina. I've heard so much about you."

All my internal alarms flare to life. My magic prickles my skin in goosebumps, but I keep a smile fixed to my face and shake Matteo's hand.

The second our hands clasp, I activate an area of my power I haven't used in five years. It's weak, but it works.

I feel an opening sensation in the center of my chest, like petals unfurling from a bud. The feeling spreads to my mind as my psychic walls part. I am a radar. A sponge. An antenna, attuned to the hopes and dreams of the person my attention falls upon.

I am an empath. And I am ready to feel what Matteo is feeling.

This marriage isn't based on love, and I don't expect Matteo to care about wedded bliss or anything like that. I figure he'll be thinking about making an advantageous match with my sister, or about the ceremony going off without a hitch.

Instead, I feel…

Greed.

The purest, darkest, most intense *wanting* I've ever sensed from another being.

I've worked with clients who wanted things before. Money, power, fame, attention. I'm used to those things in our society.

This blows all of them out of the water.

I squeeze Matteo's hand just a little tighter as we shake, and I'm hit with a clearer image of exactly what he wants.

Not just the *union* of two powerful witch families, but the *takeover.*

And then, a visual of exactly what he wants from Caro.

Demon spawn.

I fight to hold in a gasp. There is a motherfucking demon wearing Matteo's face, and he wants to beget diablitos on my sister.

I snatch my hand away and plaster a fake-ass smile on my face. "Great to meet you, Matteo!"

It's absolutely the kind of thing Crystal would've called me out on if she weren't...I don't know, in a trance? Under a spell?

Madre del Mar, they're *all* under this demon's spell.

Except for me. And my magic is a flickering flame compared to the inferno it used to be.

Compared to what I'd need it to be to fight an actual *demonio*.

Something moves in the corner of my eye and I whirl around. Two of the cameras have snuck up behind me. They're barely three feet away. My fingers curl into claws as I call forth my defensive telekinetic magic. It's an old habit, one I never kicked. Not during all the years I lived in New York, and not even after my magic abandoned me. I feel it now, pulsing in my hands. Much fainter than it used to be, but there, ready to protect me.

It's not enough though. I have to get out of here.

I turn back to my sisters. "Just remembered, I have to go to the bathroom."

One of the cameras follows as I hurry from the room, and Caro calls after me, "Cat, don't forget to enchant my wedding dress!"

Oh. Right. The dress.

I designed and crafted Caro's dress in New York, then shipped it to Florida where an old seamstress friend of mine made the alterations.

The only thing left for me to do is enchant it. Something I haven't done in five years.

The silent camera operator is still tracking me. I pick up the pace, grateful for all of Casa Cartagena's new twists and turns.

Because I am sure now that the cameras are working for the demon. Whether they're real people or not, in a trance or not, I don't know yet. But if they're unwilling participants, I can't harm them.

I need to get away and figure out how far this spell extends and what to do about it. Running full out, I take corners at random until I spy a familiar blue door set in a plain white wall.

The broom closet. Perfect.

I grab the knob and pull the door open.

My heart leaps into my throat. The shock sends my defensive power once again flaring to life.

Inside the broom closet is Diego Paz.

My nemesis.

Diego's eyes widen. He's just as shocked as I am. But there's no time for debate. The footsteps are getting closer.

I shove my way into the closet next to Diego and quietly shut the door, plunging us into darkness.

CHAPTER TWO

*I*t's quiet in the broom closet, aside from the sound of our breathing.

It's also close.

Cramped.

Heat radiates from Diego's body, warming mine.

And he smells *amazing*. Like a subtle mix of mint and sandalwood essential oils.

My heart thuds heavily in my chest at the near miss. Also, if I'm being honest, from being trapped in a tiny broom closet with *Diego Paz*.

I only got a quick look at him, but damn, talk about a glow-up.

The ultra-competitive nerd is super hot now. His dark brown hair is longer than the Caesar cuts he favored in high school, and he's got a beard and a *nose ring*. I never in a million years would've guessed he'd do that.

If it weren't for his eyes, I might not have recognized him. Those, at least, are the same. Chocolate brown, thickly lashed, and more soulful than a little snot like him deserves.

Neither of us says a word as footsteps pass near the door.

Seconds tick past and my pulse quickens, but it's only partly because of danger lurking just beyond.

The other reason is pressed to my back. Diego's body is warm, hard, and very real.

When the footsteps finally fade, I let out a breath. Time to get out of here. I reach for the door, but Diego wraps an arm around me, holding me still.

Before I can protest, he puts his mouth next to my ear and speaks in a low voice. "Don't. There's one chasing me, too."

"So there are two out there?"

"At least."

I slump a little, which makes me sag against him. It feels like he's holding me up, and I don't like it.

No, that's a lie. I like it very much. But I stiffen my spine anyway.

"Does this mean you aren't under the demon's spell?" I mutter.

"Would I be hiding in a broom closet if I were?"

The sarcasm in his tone makes me snippy. "I don't know what you like to do with your free time, Diego."

He sighs. "How do I know *you're* not entranced?"

"Because I'm *also* hiding in a broom closet."

"Touché."

I tilt my ear toward the door and listen closely. "Do you think those things are gone?"

"No idea. But we shouldn't take any chances."

"Right." Something presses against me and I suck in a breath. "Diego?"

"Hmm?"

"Get your hand off my butt."

A long moment passes before he answers, sounding mildly embarrassed. "That's not my hand."

My face heats, and I'm suddenly glad for the dark. "Oh."

"You have a great ass. Now keep still."

He shifts behind me, and my heart rate kicks up. In alarm or arousal, I'm not sure. "Why, what are you doing back there?"

"Relax. I'm going to cast a light so we can see. Close your eyes."

Normally I'd keep arguing with him, but I don't want Diego to know my magical abilities aren't what they used to be. So I close my eyes, blocking out even the little bit of light seeping around the edges of the door. Diego's arms encircle me loosely. I know exactly what spell he's doing. It's simple, one of the first taught to children. I'm not sure I can even do it anymore, but I imagine Diego's hands moving in the dark. When I open my eyes, a small yellow orb floats in the air just above my head, casting a faint, friendly light over us.

Taking care not to jostle the brooms whose home we've invaded, I turn so I can finally get a good look at Diego's face.

And praise Luna, what a face it is. Strong nose, serious brows and a jaw that's filled out since I last saw him. Yeah, my childhood rival is all grown up now, and sexy as Sol.

I clear my throat. "So, um, how did you end up in this closet?"

"Same as you, I expect. I was looking for my parents when one of the cameras started following me."

"Your parents?"

"They texted me to meet them here."

"We should assume they're also ensorcelled, like mine."

"I think that's a safe bet."

"So what do we do about it?"

"First things first, we have to get out of here."

"Great, but where do we go? We have no idea who summoned the demon. It could be one of the other familias. Maybe someone who wants to stop the consolidation of power. I mean, the wedding."

The corner of his mouth quirks in a smile. "You're right. We need neutral ground."

I groan. "I hope you don't mean what I think you mean."

His tone is tinged with humor. "What do you have against The

16

Crone's Nest Inn? It has better wards than anywhere else on the island."

"Is your great-uncle still the proprietor?"

Diego's grin is full blown. Somehow, it lights up the small space even more. "What's wrong with Tío Nestor?"

"Nothing. I love your tío Nestor. But he's…"

"A lot?"

"That's putting it mildly. You know he's going to demand I design him another cape."

"He still talks about the first one you made."

"I've made him *twenty*. How do we know Nestor isn't involved?"

"Tío Nestor stays out of family drama."

"Pretty sure a demon possessing your brother days before his wedding to my sister goes well beyond the category of drama. This is a straight-up scandal."

"We'll deal with the fallout later. For now we have to figure out how to get out of here."

Crystal's muffled voice cuts him off. "Cat? Where are you, Cat?"

I let out a startled squeak. "Shit, it's Crystal."

"Casita, find Catalina," Crystal calls out.

The closet door shudders.

"Thanks a lot, Casita," I mutter.

Diego's brows draw together in a scowl, and he looks so fierce and dangerous and, okay, yes, *sexy*, that I wouldn't put it past him to blast my sister if he thought she were a threat.

I tap Diego's shoulder to get his attention. "I'm going to kiss you."

His eyebrows leap up, and the corners of his mouth curve.

"Odd reaction, but I'm not opposed."

"It's just to give us a cover story for why we're in this closet."

He opens his arms to me. "Do your worst."

I step into the space he's made, bringing us even closer than we already were. I cup his face, and his hands land on my waist. Crystal's footsteps come nearer.

We're out of time. No turning back now.

Raising my chin, I gently pull his face down to mine. I mean for it to be like a stage kiss. Just pretend, you know? But a second before our lips meet, mine part on an indrawn breath. And then his mouth is on mine and before I know it, our tongues are touching. Tasting. Licking. A thrill races through me, and I lean closer. His arms tighten around my waist and then—

The door swings open and I jump. Somehow, I'd forgotten that we were only kissing to create this exact moment. My face heats as we break apart, and I don't have to pretend to be surprised when I see Crystal standing there.

She clamps a hand on my wrist and drags me out of the closet. "I found you! Just in time to record your interview."

"Crystal, did you not just see me kissing Diego? In a closet?"

She blinks rapidly. Her wide smile falters, then turns into something closer to a smirk. "The maid of honor and the best man hooking up before the wedding? Bit of a cliche, Cat. But hey, if the broom fits, ride it."

Now *that* sounds much more like Crystal. I shrug, and try to appear sheepish. "Hey, there's no fighting chemistry, if you know what I'm saying."

She gives me a lewd wink. "Oh, I know…"

Her eyes widen and her jaw goes slack. She finishes the sentence in a bubbly voice. "I know…that you have to film your interview!"

Oh, hex no. There's no way on Tierra that I'm letting those cameras catch me.

I grab Diego's hand and give Crystal a bright smile. "Well, Diego and I are gonna go make out some more. Just can't get enough of this hot nerd action. Maybe we'll do the interview later?"

Diego draws me away from her just as two camera operators

come into view. We duck around the corner and watch as the cameras zero in on Crystal. From this vantage point, I can just make out her face.

"Oh, is it time for another interview?" Crystal smiles wide and tosses her hair over her shoulder. Before she can say another word, the camera lenses glow and Crystal's expression turns dazed. Her eyes are unfocused, staring into space, and her jaw hangs open.

I cover my mouth to stifle a gasp. *I knew it.* The cameras are reinforcing the demon's spell. Probably keeping an eye on all of us too.

Diego pulls me down the hallway before the cameras can come after us again. "That was close," he says.

"Too close."

"Can you teleport us out?"

"Um, not exactly."

"Coño." That angular jaw of his tightens. "Until our families are united, I can't teleport within your family's wards."

"We should've grabbed a couple brooms. They were right there."

"Too late now."

"Cat?" a voice calls. It's my mother.

"Diego? Where are you?" And that's my dad.

"They're looking for us. Come on." Diego grabs my hand and we start to run.

We don't have time to get lost, so I voice a plea to the house. "Casita? A little help here? We need an exit."

A door swings open in front of us and we charge through. It takes us down a long passageway I recognize. We burst through a side door and make a run for the property line. The second we pass through the wards, Diego pulls me into his arms. There's a lurching sensation, like when you're walking downstairs and you miss a step. I shut my eyes as the ground drops away, and don't open them until I feel solid earth beneath my feet once more.

We're both breathing hard, staring at each other from too close. Diego's still holding me, and I don't move away.

Running for our lives distracted me from what we did, but now that we're safe?

All I can think about is that I just kissed him. I kissed Diego Paz.

And I liked it.

CHAPTER THREE

*B*efore I can decide whether to kiss Diego again or push him away, a loud voice interrupts. "¡Oye, muchachos! ¡Ven acá!"

Diego releases me and waves at his uncle, Nestor De León.

Tío Nestor is the proprietor of The Crone's Nest Inn, the only bed and breakfast on the island. He's a fashion icon, even by Isla Bruja standards. He has an incredible collection of wigs, capes, and bedazzled suits, and I don't think I've ever seen him wear the same combo twice. He was one of my earliest patrons when I started my business, for which I'll always be grateful.

But he's also a talker. Once you get him going, good luck escaping the conversation or getting a word in edgewise.

Diego snaps his fingers, and a large rolling suitcase appears at his side.

"Where's your luggage?" he asks.

"In my room at my parents' house."

"We'll get it after the rehearsal dinner."

Diego grabs the suitcase handle with his left hand, then takes my hand with his right, leading me toward The Crone's Nest. It's a cozy building painted a cheery yellow and nestled behind a row of palm trees. But like all the other structures on Isla Bruja, it's much bigger and more eclectic on the inside.

I shake our joined hands and hiss, "What are you doing, Diego?"

"Selling the story."

"What story?"

"The one you told your sister. Best man hooking up with the maid of honor?"

"It was the only thing I could think of in the moment," I grumble.

"It's brilliant in its simplicity. And it's just what we need to make everyone leave us alone until we fix things."

"Should we tell Nestor what's going on?"

"No. Don't tell anyone. Tío Nestor can't keep a secret to save his life, and we don't know who to trust yet."

"How do I know I can trust you?"

"Cat. Come on," he says quietly. "You know you can trust me."

And despite the terror of the situation, he's right. Aside from my parents and sisters, I get Diego better than I get anyone else on Isla Bruja. You know that adage, "Know your friends well and your enemies better"? I took that to heart in high school. It had been my mission to completely understand Diego, the better to take him down.

We pass through the inn's wards and Nestor greets us with hugs and kisses. He's wearing what look like turquoise silk pajamas, beautifully embroidered with peacocks and bougainvillea, and a platinum blond Mae West wig.

"To what do I owe the visit?" Nestor asks, putting an arm around each of us and leading us inside.

Diego replies easily. "We wanted to see if you have any rooms available."

"Pues, deja me ver." Nestor leads us to the front desk, which looks like it belongs in the lobby of a haunted 1940s hotel, aside from the 12-foot-tall glittering glass mosaic of Celia Cruz towering behind it.

Nestor perches a pair of gold half-moon reading glasses on the end of his nose and flips open a large leatherbound book. He eyes us over the tops of the glasses. "You're not staying con sus familias?"

Before I can answer, Diego leans an elbow on the counter and lowers his voice conspiratorially. "We would, but it can be hard to find privacy around them. ¿Tú sabes?"

Nestor gives him a knowing nod. "Ay sí. Yo sé eso. I hear you loud and clear, mi sobrinito."

Fighting the urge to roll my eyes, I tune them out and fiddle with the belongings in my purse while they make arrangements. Then I hear Nestor say, "Bueno, here's your key."

Key. He said *key*, singular. Not *keys*.

I look up in alarm. "Only one room?"

Nestor spreads his hands and looks almost apologetic, but not quite. The corners of his mouth twitch like he's trying not to laugh. "There are so many people coming to witness the wedding of the century, all the other rooms are booked."

Diego turns to me. "Is that a problem, mi corazón?"

My heart pounds at the term of endearment, but I shake my head. "No, no problem. Not at all."

This is part of our cover story, right? It doesn't have to be a big deal.

Sharing a room with Diego, my sexy nemesis, doesn't have to be a big deal.

Diego accepts the single key and I give myself a pep talk as we head upstairs.

Be cool, Cat. Act normal. Say something. "So, uh, what room did we get?"

Diego, who appears completely unbothered by the situation, jingles the skeleton key with its coffin-shaped keychain. "I'll give you three guesses."

I groan. "Oh for the love of Luna. Not the Vampire Suite!"

"It's the only vacant room."

"But it's so…"

"Funereal? Macabre? Depressing?"

"*Drab.*"

Diego unlocks the door and I peer inside.

"See what I mean? Why is it all black? Would it hurt to put a pop of red somewhere? Stop looking at me like that, Diego."

"You do realize *you're* wearing all-black, right?"

"I live in New York City now. I was planning to change, but got sidetracked by a power-hungry demon. In hindsight, the fact that my mother didn't comment on my outfit should've told me immediately that she wasn't herself."

"Hey, at least the bed isn't a coffin."

"Good point." There's an enormous four-poster bed in the center of the room, complete with black hanging drapes. A lot could go on in that bed.

Wait, what am I thinking? This is *Diego*. Nothing is going to go on in that bed. I look for somewhere else to sit and head for the black velvet fainting couch along the wall. "All right, since we're here, we might as well get comfortable."

"And figure out how to exorcise a demon." Diego stores his luggage by the door and takes a seat in a black leather armchair.

"What if we try to snap my mom out of it?" I suggest. "She's an expert at exorcisms."

"Too risky. It might alert the demon that we're onto it."

"We should make it a competition, for old time's sake. See who can banish the demon first."

"*Or* we could work together." He sounds exasperated.

I lounge on the fainting couch, which is surprisingly comfortable. "Yeah, I guess we could do that too."

"We only have three days. Including today."

"If we don't get this demon out of your brother, it'll have access to the full power of both families. Not to mention, Matteo and Caro's children will be literal demon spawn. Babysitting our niblings would be absolute hell."

"I'm a little more concerned about my brother's quality of life, but sure. Babysitting. Let's worry about that."

"Actually, I didn't want to ask but…"

"No, I'm not dating anyone."

"That's not what I was going to ask you!" I sputter.

"Sorry. Continue. Are *you* dating anyone?"

"No, I'm not. Stay on track." I take a deep breath to un-fluster myself. "Are we sure Matteo didn't invite this demon into himself? It's happened at some of the other enclaves."

Diego shakes his head. "Matteo wouldn't do that. He's way too stubborn to let anyone else pull his strings."

"Except he's letting your mom push him into marrying Caro."

"I'm not saying he isn't ambitious, but he would never hand over total control of his body. He'd be too worried about the demon skipping leg day."

"Well, thank Sol for your brother's gym routine."

Diego ignores my sarcastic remark. "Let's brainstorm a plan of attack."

"Simplest is usually best."

"Like your idea that we should pretend to be hooking up," he says, and I don't think I'm imagining the spark of heat in his eyes.

"I don't know that I'd call it an *idea*," I mumble. "It was spur of the moment."

"You were always good at thinking on your feet."

"I—thank you." The easy praise makes my cheeks warm, but Diego keeps going.

"How did you know Matteo was possessed?"

"I used my empathic powers. The same ones I use when I'm designing clothes."

"Huh." Those dark brows draw together. "I thought you used alchemy for that?"

"On the fabric, yes. But I start out by tapping into the person's hopes and dreams for the event. I take how they want to feel and enchant the garment to help them achieve their goal."

His expression softens. "Hey, you remember when you made my mom that dress?"

"How could I forget? It's the only reason you won the valedictorian spot."

"No doubt. Well, I never told you, but it was an amazing design. I don't think I've ever seen her so happy, before or since."

"Oh. That's…that's nice to hear. Wait a second, how did *you* know? About Matteo."

He scoffs. "Trust me, I know my brother. It was clear something was wrong, so I did a subtle revelation spell that showed me he's possessed."

"Makes sense. Your spells are nearly undetectable."

His lips curve. "Was that a compliment, Cat?"

"Don't let it go to your head," I mumble.

"All right," he continues. "You said you used your empathic powers to read the demon inside Matteo. So what does it want?"

I shiver at the memory. "*Power.* I've never felt anybody want something that badly."

"Well, it'll have shitloads of it if we can't stop the wedding. Got any ideas?"

"I'm…a little rusty."

His brow creases. "You don't use magic in New York?"

"Never."

"Never?" He sounds incredulous. "Don't you miss it?"

"I…yeah. Sometimes. Anyway, I'd probably try a purification spell first. Demon possession is like an infection, or a corruption."

"My thoughts exactly. A simple but well executed purification spell might knock it out of Matteo's body."

"It's worth a shot. And if it doesn't work, we'll break out the big guns."

He winces. "Can we not use gun metaphors? I'd prefer not to

kill my brother. I'm very happy not having the pressure that comes with being the oldest."

"Sorry. Let's compile the ingredients and work on the incantation."

"I'm sure Tío Nestor has everything we need in the kitchen."

"How are we going to explain that? He'll guess that we're doing a purification spell and want to know why."

"That's where you come in, mi corazón."

I groan. "Oh no."

"Just get Tío Nestor talking about his cape collection—"

"Diego, do not do this to me."

"And I'll get everything we need for the spell. Easy as that."

I jab a finger in his direction. "You are cruel and unusual."

"Only for you, babe."

And then he winks.

My stomach somersaults. Was Diego always this much of a flirt? I'm sure I would remember that. And I'd certainly remember if he had this kind of effect on me before.

Cheeks burning, I head downstairs to find Nestor. When I ask if he's obtained anything new since I was last in town, his eyes light up. He hurries me to his private suite, which has an entire room just for his capes.

Nestor makes the introductions. "This burgundy silk with the ostrich features is Tonya, and this emerald green beauty with the embroidered basilisk is Flavio."

I respond accordingly to each cape, but when I spot some of my own creations hanging among them, I feel a twinge of grief.

After Nestor's done introducing me to his new "bebés," I drag myself back to the Vampire Suite where Diego greets me with a grin.

"How many new capes?" he asks.

"*Fourteen.*" I flop face down on the bed and try to ignore the fact that Diego is wearing nothing but a black towel tied around his waist. My voice is muffled as I speak into the bedding. "Did you get everything?"

"I did. Can you prep the herbs while I take a salt bath?"

"Fine." I wait until I hear the bathroom door close before I sit up again. Is the man trying to fluster me on purpose? And just how many tattoos does he have?

Despite my reduced access to magic, I still remember the rituals. Ritualistic magic requires more prep work and study, as opposed to natural magic like telekinesis, which demands hours of practice to hone. Since Diego will be the one casting the spell, he takes a purifying sea salt bath while I grind bay leaves, broad leaf thyme, and culantro with a mortar and pestle. The herbaceous scent simultaneously makes me hungry and reminds me of home.

Once Diego's out of the bath—and fully dressed—he spreads a beaded mat across the dresser and lays El Padre, the fifth card of the Isla Bruja tarot deck, in the center. We place a white jar candle on top of the card and surround it with carved wooden symbols of our deities. La Luna, the moon and mother. El Sol, the sun and father. Tierra and Mar, earth and sea, are their children. And the fifth, who is never named except in ritual and prayer, el Espíritu, the spirit.

After burning enough of the candle for the top layer of wax to melt, Diego sprinkles in the herbs I've crushed. We'll use this to conduct the spell during the rehearsal dinner tonight.

We spend the rest of the time working on the incantation. Words have power, and we want to get it right. But sometimes we detour into intellectual discussions about spell structure and magical theory, and it's nice to have someone to debate these topics with. For the past five years, I've completely shut off this part of my life, and I missed it.

I also have to admit Diego and I are getting along better than we ever did before. I don't know how to handle this new side of him, but it's kind of…pleasant to be working *with* him rather than *against* him.

Neither of us brings up the kiss.

Once we have everything prepared for the spell, we get ready to head back to Casa Cartagena.

Diego passes me a protective charm to keep in my pocket.

"How long have you been back?" he asks.

"Just arrived today. Had to finish up Fashion Week."

"Me too. Well, not Fashion Week, but we debuted a new menu."

"Menu?"

"At my restaurant. In Miami."

"Oh. I didn't know that's what you were doing now."

"You mean you haven't been Internet stalking me?" His tone is teasing.

"No! I mean…not in a while, anyway."

"I'm offended. What kind of nemesis are you?"

I put my hands on my hips. "Don't tell me you've been keeping tabs on *me* all this time."

He leans in close and tilts my chin up with one finger. "Of course I have…*Salutatorian.*"

As we leave the inn, I'm fuming.

Forget the demon. Tonight, I'm going to kill Diego while he sleeps.

CHAPTER FOUR

*T*he rehearsal dinner is held in the ballroom at Casa Cartagena. Since my mother planned this part, the tablecloths are orange, and the centerpieces are outrageously tacky explosions of tropical flowers, which match the French Baroque style of the ballroom not even a little bit. The Paz De León and Cartagena Vargas families are here, along with aunts, uncles, cousins, and a catering squad. The room is positively teeming with camera operators.

Diego takes my hand and leans close to my ear. "We stick together. There's no telling who's bewitched or not."

"Right. Let's get those symbols chalked."

But before we can start the spell, we have to say hello to everyone.

It's hard to tell who's affected and who isn't. Everyone seems a little distracted, but that could just be from the open bar. Some relatives are hyper focused on procuring camera time, but that could just be vanity. They seem, for the most part, like themselves, aside from the occasional far-off look in their eyes.

They are not, however, distracted enough to miss that Diego is glued to my side the entire night.

"Ay mira, qué preciosa. Look at you two!"

"Qué guapo. Such a handsome couple you make."

"A double wedding, huh? I'm only giving one gift!"

And so on.

It only gets worse after we manage to hide the candle under one of the unoccupied tables. Diego lights it with magic, and I say a prayer that we don't accidentally burn the whole place down. But now we have to chalk five symbols around the room without being interrupted.

The plan is for Diego to use my body to block what he's doing. People will think we're necking in the corner, and hopefully leave us alone. One, two, three, four, five symbols, and then we'll be done. Uncomplicated in theory.

Super fucking complicated in practice.

For one thing, I've been trying all day not to think about how good Diego felt pressed up against me in the closet. Or about how nice he smelled. Or how that *wasn't his hand* touching my ass.

Okay, I'm a liar. I've been thinking about that part all. Day. Long.

It's even worse in a brightly lit ballroom with both of our families as an audience.

In the southeast corner of the room, Diego presses my back against the wall and slides his arm around my waist. With his mouth next to my ear, he whispers, "First symbol. El Mar."

I feel his left hand moving against my lower back as he draws the symbol in chalk. He breathes the associated incantation as if he's whispering sweet nothings, and I don't have to pretend to be swooning. We're chest to chest, pelvis to pelvis. His closeness and the flutter of his lips against the shell of my ear is doing things to me. Dark, delicious things.

It's all I can do to keep an eye out, and I struggle to find words when I see my younger sister Cleo approaching.

"Someone's coming," I say on a gasp.

Diego's hand stills. "I'm going to put my hand on your butt."

31

I bite my lip in anticipation of his touch, but out loud, I only say, "Go for it."

His hot palm lands on my ass, his fingers molding around the curve. I narrowly resist the urge to tell him to squeeze. You know, to make this more believable. That's all.

Then he swirls his tongue against the side of my neck, and I nearly jump out of my own skin.

Cleo stops in front of us and props a hand on her hip like she's a model striking a pose. She's twenty and acts like she's too cool for this world. I wonder how much of that is because I left when she was fifteen, and she stepped up to take my place as the family's golden goose. With her sharp cheekbones and natural haughtiness, she became the belle of the Isla Bruja balls, which made my mom hostess supreme.

If you thought the presence of my younger sister would be like a bucket of ice water over my libido, you'd be wrong. When Diego lifts his head to look at Cleo, I want to drag his mouth back to me so he can continue whatever he was just doing with his tongue.

Cleo's expression is bored, but still somehow dazed. She's clearly under the demon's spell.

"Abuela's looking for you, Cat," she drawls.

"Um, I'm a little busy here. Do you know what she wants?"

Cleo shrugs. "You know how she is."

I do. My grandmother is a force of nature. She's the queen of glamours, and she specializes in dance magic. She has a way of commanding attention and influencing people I've always admired.

I am also completely incapable of saying no to her.

Cleo leaves, and Diego releases me.

"We're running out of time," I tell him. "Did you finish the symbol?"

"I did."

"Good. We have to get the others done before my grandmother catches us."

"Next up is Tierra. Head to the southwest corner."

This time, Diego urges me to prop my butt on the edge of one of the tables. He uses my ass to shield what he's drawing.

His other hand hovers near my waist. "Hand under your shirt?" he asks, seeking permission.

I hold back a moan. "Do it."

He slides his right hand beneath the fabric of my tank top and up my back. The brush of his fingers on my bare skin makes me shiver. He stills.

"You okay?"

I nod. "Yeah. Fine."

"Don't be nervous."

Nervous? Ha. Turned on beyond belief is more like it.

"I'm not. Don't worry. Keep going."

He leans in and presses his face into my hair, so our relatives don't see that he's reciting the incantation for Tierra. He's bending over me at an awkward angle that's probably hurting his back. Good little partner in crime that I am, I part my thighs and put my arms around him, pulling him closer. I catch a slight hitch in his breathing, but he continues the incantation. His fingers move against my butt as he draws on the table.

My pulse beats thickly in my throat, and it takes me a moment to realize Diego has stopped speaking. His left hand has gone still, the symbol complete, but he hasn't moved it away from my ass.

"Are you done?" I ask.

"Yeah, I just…need a minute."

Before I can ask why, he drops his forehead to my shoulder and tilts his pelvis away from me.

Oh. *That's* why.

Well hex, it's nice to know I'm not the only one who's a mess of hormones tonight.

We get through the symbols for la Luna in the northwest and el Sol in the northeast, despite the camera operators closing in. It takes us a while to get to the northern point of the room, where

Diego will mark the final symbol for el Espíritu. I tell him to go do it on his own, but he refuses to leave my side.

We're pretending to make out when I spot my grandmother charging toward us. I let out a horrified gasp and shove Diego off me.

"Hurry and finish it!"

Diego rushes through the rest of the incantation, marking the symbol in chalk on the wall. When he's done, we wait a beat.

Nothing happens.

"Did you feel the spell take hold?" I ask.

His brows pinch together. "No. Something's wrong."

Our gazes fly to the table where we hid the candle, just in time to see one of the caterers walking away with it. A faint trail of smoke billows from the wick, the only remnants of the extinguished flame.

"Fuck," we say in unison. And there's nothing else we can do, because my grandmother is here.

Abuela is barely five feet tall and at least eighty years old, although it's hard to say because she lies about her age and glamours her skin to look younger. She's wearing one of my designs, a flowing lilac gown with puffy translucent sleeves and what look like hundreds of fluttering butterflies alighted on the fabric. It's stunning, and something inside me twists as I remember how good it felt to create beauty with my magic.

Abuela clucks her tongue. "Maid of honor and best man. Nice to see you both bothered to show up."

I sputter in protest. "Abuela, we were working."

"Ohhh, ¿claro que sí?" She doesn't sound impressed. "Pues, since you both have so much free time on your hands now, here's a list of remaining chores for the wedding."

I glance at the paper she hands me. "When are we supposed to do all this?"

"Tonight. Get to work."

She gives us the evil eye, then stalks away.

34

Diego and I read over the list. It's long, and includes stuff like "double check chair count," "confirm cake delivery time," and "rearrange seating in third white and blue sitting room."

Diego crosses his arms. "Can we say no?"

"Trust me, you don't want to say no to my grandmother. And she's right, we have been delinquent in our duties." I sigh. "It'll go faster if we split up."

"No way. What if the cameras catch us? We're safer together."

I shrug. "We'd better get started then."

By the time Diego teleports us back to the B&B with my luggage, all traces of the arousal I felt earlier have been extinguished by exhaustion. I stumble when we land in front of The Crone's Nest. Diego catches my arm to steady me, but there's nothing sexy about the gesture. He looks just as tired as I feel, with heavy shadows beneath his eyes.

"Well, that was a bust," he says, his tone dejected.

"We'll try again tomorrow night during the bachelor party." I try to sound reassuring, but I don't think I manage it.

Once inside our room, we pause by the door, taking in the furniture. After a long look at the bed, Diego heads for the fainting couch. "I'll sleep on this. You can take the bed."

"Diego…"

"I don't mind, Cat."

"Well, I do. Look, this bed is enormous. And we're adults. There's no reason for you to be uncomfortable all night when there's so much space. And I need you to be sharp enough to take on a demon tomorrow. Just sleep in the bed…with me."

If he notices I falter on the last two words, he doesn't comment. After one last look at the fainting couch, he gives up the argument. "You're right. The demon has to be powerful if it's managing a spell of this magnitude.

"Let's just get some rest, okay? We'll regroup in the morning."

We take turns in the bathroom, which appears to be carved entirely out of black marble, and slide into the bed on opposite sides. There's still enough space that we could fit a whole other person between us.

But I don't want someone else there. I want to be closer to Diego.

The impulse surprises me. I wasn't attracted to him when we were in school. Had I noticed his pretty brown eyes? Sure. But I'd been so absorbed in taking him down a peg, that hadn't mattered.

Yes, Diego is objectively hot now, but it's not the only thing drawing me to him. He's more confident, less of a show-off, less argumentative.

As for me, I don't feel the need to constantly one-up him or prove that I'm right and he's wrong.

Maybe we've both grown up.

I'm overthinking this, trying to find a logical explanation for how he makes me feel inside, when the truth is...

I just want him.

My body responds to Diego in a way that it hasn't for anyone else. At the party, every time he pressed against me, or slid a hand over my waist, or whispered in my ear, it didn't matter that it was for show, or that he was talking about magical symbols and spells.

All that mattered was that he was touching me, and I didn't want him to stop.

He rolls over. The rustle of the sheet sounds loud and intimate in the dark, and I feel the slight tug on my end of the blanket.

"Goodnight, Cat."

His voice gives me goosebumps. If only I weren't too tired to enjoy them.

"Goodnight, Diego."

CHAPTER FIVE

*L*ucky for me, my sister Crystal planned the bachelorette party, and even in her half-trance state, she's managing the guests—and the open bar—well enough that she doesn't notice me sneaking out. The cameras have followed us to the club, and they're a little harder to ditch. It takes me three trips to the bathroom before I'm able to lose my tail and head to the other club where Diego is keeping an eye on his brother.

Diego knows the club owner, another brujo, who gives him access to a side door. He meets me there and lets me inside.

That morning, Diego was already gone when I woke up, sparing us any awkwardness. He'd left a note saying he was going to borrow some spell books from Nestor, and he returned with the books and coffee as I was blow drying my hair. We spent the rest of the day flipping through old grimoires and determining our next course of action for expelling the demon wearing Matteo's face. It was like studying before a big test, but with much higher stakes.

Once upon a time, I thought test scores were the highest stakes imaginable. Life has shown me otherwise.

We've decided to attempt a banishment spell, something tried and true. After returning to Casa Cartagena and raiding my mom's supplies, we packed everything into my purse and split up to join the parties.

Since it'll be suspicious for the maid of honor to show up at the groom's bachelor party, the plan is for me to cast a glamour over myself to pose as a waitress.

There's just one problem. I still haven't told Diego my powers are mostly dormant.

Diego draws me into the coat room after paying the attendant a hundred bucks to take a five minute break.

"All right, Cat. It's glamour time."

"Oh yeah. Uh, can you cast it on me?"

He snorts. "You think I would've endured middle school with this nose if I had any kind of glamour skills?"

"You grew into your nose. And besides, you managed to pass all the glamour exams with flying colors."

"By the skin of my teeth. I definitely don't have the skills to cast a glamour on someone else. Come on, your grandma is one of the best glamourists alive. And I still remember how you convinced everyone at school you'd dyed your hair pink for a full week. This should be a piece of cake for you."

"About that…"

He ducks his head, looking at me with concern. "What's wrong?"

"It's possible…that I don't…have magic anymore."

His eyes widen in disbelief. "You what?"

I take a deep breath and finally let the truth out. "I can't access my magic. It's why I left Isla Bruja five years ago. I burned out. Physically, emotionally, magically…you name it."

"It's really gone?" His voice is hushed.

"Not completely. It's been coming back slowly, like a hum under my skin. But I haven't used it for serious spellcasting in years."

"I didn't know that could happen." There's compassion in his tone, and it makes it easier to tell him the rest.

"By the time I left Isla Bruja, I was working so hard, I was barely eating, neglecting everything except the work. I'd spend all day locked in my workroom, completely focused on the fabric and the patterns and the enchantments. I was striving so hard to be the best and then one day…it was gone."

Diego takes me in his arms, his movements gentle. "Lo siento, mi corazón. I didn't know."

"I didn't want to tell you," I mumble.

"Why not?"

I give a light laugh. "Admit a weakness to my nemesis? Never."

He smiles and looks deeply into my eyes. "Am I really still your nemesis?"

I let out a long breath. "I guess not."

"So what am I, Cat, if not your rival?"

"I…I'm not sure." The words come out breathy.

He moves even closer and his voice deepens. "What do you want me to be?"

I'm saved from having to answer when the coat check attendant returns. I finally take a good look at her. We both have long dark hair and similar coloring, but she's wearing thick-framed glasses and a pink velvet headband.

I pull two hundred-dollar bills out of my wallet and hold them out to her. "Can I borrow your headband and glasses for the night?"

Her eyes go wide at the sight of the money. She yanks off the accessories and hands them to me. "Here. Have fun."

I give her the money and put on the rented disguise. The world is a little blurry, but not terribly so.

Diego grins. "Cute look. I like it."

The coat check attendant sidles up to me and says in a stage whisper, "Just try not to get any stains on the hairband, okay? It's my favorite."

I balk. *"Stains?"*

Stifling a laugh, Diego leads me away. "I'm pretty sure she thinks we want them for something kinky."

"What, like role-play?"

"Who knows?"

A million thoughts run through my head in the space of a second. "Are you into that?"

He taps the corner of my glasses and gives me a slow smile. "I think I could be."

I think I could be too, but I don't say so.

We stop by the bar, where Diego orders a drink. While the bartender is distracted, I snag a circular tray and a little black apron from behind the bar. I tie the apron around my waist and transfer the spell supplies and my purse into the pockets. When Diego brings his drink over, I pop it on the tray. Waitress costume complete!

Diego uncaps a vial of lavender oil and dabs some on the side of my neck before doing the same to himself. I close my eyes and breathe in slowly, letting the piney herbal scent overwhelm my senses. It's imperative that we stay calm while casting the banishing spell, and hopefully the lavender will help.

"Ready?" he asks me.

"As I'll ever be."

I start to walk away from the bar, but Diego stops me. He grabs the drink, sets it aside, and pulls me in for a kiss.

It's over before I even realize it began, and I stare up at him, blinking in shock.

"What was that for?"

"Because I'm worried about you," he growls. "And I know it won't do any good to tell you to leave and let me handle this."

"You're right, it won't."

"But the fact remains, we're about to face off against a demon, and we might not walk away from this. I couldn't do that with-out...shit, I'm sorry, I should've asked to kiss you first."

"Diego." I put a hand to his chest. "I'm glad you kissed me."

A brief smile flashes across his face, and then his dark brows come together in determination. "We'll do it again after we survive this."

He means *if* we survive this, but I don't correct him. I just nod and follow him to the VIP lounge he rented out for Matteo's bachelor party.

Honestly, it's a shame Matteo is checked out, because this is the Brujo Bro party to end all Brujo Bro parties. Diego's two younger brothers are getting lap dances, his cousins are downing shots, and all of Matteo's other friends crowd around the stage where a man and a woman pull off some impressive pole dancing routines.

Noticeably absent are the camera operators. I nudge Diego with my elbow. "No cameras."

His eyes narrow as he scans the scene. "I noticed that too. I figured the demon doesn't think they're needed, since he's present."

"Or maybe it's stretched too thin? Between keeping our families under surveillance, along with the cameras at Caro's party, the spell must require a ton of energy to maintain."

"Let's hope that's true. If the demon is weakened, then maybe we stand a chance of pulling this off."

He's right. It's dangerous to work strong magic around humans, away from the safety of Isla Bruja. And if it's risky for us, maybe it's risky for the demon, too.

Diego's hand brushes mine, and I take more comfort from the soft touch than I should.

"I get it, you know," he says quietly.

"Get what?"

"Why you left. Isla Bruja can be…stifling. All the expectations of family and community. I went away, but then I missed it. That's why I live and work in Miami. Close, but not too close."

"Huh." What a novel concept.

I spot one of my ex-boyfriends throwing money onto the stage and duck my head. I want to explore this conversation more, but I can't chance any of these idiotas recognizing me, or our plan is ruined. "Go get him, Diego."

I wait by the entrance to the VIP area while Diego goes to speak to his brother.

To the demon.

It doesn't take long, and a few moments later, Diego brings Matteo over to me.

I lower my head and gesture with my hand. "Right this way, gentlemen."

They chat as I lead them to the private room where we're going to perform the banishment spell.

Matteo looks around, like he's suspicious. "Where are we going?"

"To a private room," Diego tells him. "I set up that performance you said you wanted. Just like I promised I would."

"…Right."

We reach the door, and Diego and Matteo go in. There's no one else in this stretch of hallway, since Diego rented out all the rooms. We don't want a human audience for what we're about to do.

I wait outside the room and remove a black candle from the pocket of my borrowed apron. It's been anointed with coconut oil, and Diego carved a banishment symbol into it. In my other hand, I hold a small pouch of black salt. Diego has already been inside to lay a salt circle around the room. All I have to do is complete the circle. Due to the layout of the room, the only choice is to trap ourselves in the circle with the demon, then perform the banishment spell from inside.

It's not a perfect plan, but we're running out of time and it's the best we've got. The wedding is tomorrow night.

I close my eyes and take a few deep, soothing breaths. In. And out. In. And out. Diego's the one who will be casting the spell, but

I don't want to ruin it by bringing negative energy into the circle with me.

I'm scared, though. Diego's right, I shouldn't be here. I don't have my magic anymore, and I'm more of a liability than an asset.

But I can't let him do this alone either. I have to help however I can.

Instead of worrying about the odds of our survival, I focus on our kiss by the bar. It was brief, just a press of Diego's lips to mine, and I want more. Much more. All the feelings he stirred up in me during the rehearsal dinner come roaring back, and I let them replace the fear.

There's a scratching sound on the wall, and I open my eyes. That's the signal. With one more deep breath, I push open the door and enter.

The private room is just what you'd expect it to be. Square, with dim red lighting. Cushioned benches line three walls, and a square platform sits in the center. Is it a table? A stage? Maybe both. Low music with a heavy pulsing beat pumps through the speakers.

Matteo sprawls on the bench facing the door. Diego stands off to the side. As I enter the room, I lower my head demurely and pour the salt across the threshold. The second the circle is complete, a thrum of magic goes through the room, and I know we all feel it.

I spin around and thrust the candle out. With a flick of his fingers, Diego forces the wick into flame. But before he can even begin the incantation, the demon lets out a mighty roar and leaps over the table at him.

I scramble out of the way as they grapple on the floor. Diego attempts to use spells on the demon, but I can tell he's holding back. It's his brother's body, after all.

My magic is close, humming along my skin like a live wire. It's faint, but it's there. I start to recite the incantation, glad that we worked on it together, grateful that I can remember it despite my fear. But the demon throws Diego aside and rounds on me instead.

Matteo's perfect face is distorted with rage, and his voice holds an inhuman growl. "You think you can get rid of me with a little salt and a candle? Your families are mine. Their power is mine. And there's not a damned thing you can—"

Diego tackles him from behind, cutting off the tirade. I struggle to continue the incantation, but they're getting closer to me. Climbing onto a bench, I dart away from them, but Matteo grabs my ankle. I tumble onto the cushions, dropping the candle in the process. It falls to the floor and rolls into the shadows cast by the stage.

I don't see a flame. It's gone out.

Matteo heaves Diego off him and shoves him toward the door. I feel the energy of the salt circle drop. Diego's foot must have broken it.

Our plan is ruined.

The demon charges for me and I throw my hands out. It's self-defense, an old habit. I don't expect anything to happen but suddenly my magic is *here*. Now. Right when I need it most. My hands are almost on fire with it, but it's not just my telekinesis that's at the ready. It's *all* of it. My shields are blown away and I feel within me an awareness of all the fabric in this room, of the energies that make up our deities.

Outside, the moon is nearly full. La Luna has always been my guardian, and she is here now, filling me up with pure potential.

Pure power.

The apron ties skitter from around my waist and fly through the air at Matteo's thick neck. They encircle twice, the ends twisting themselves into a binding knot.

I sense the second the knot is complete, and I shout, "En el nombre de la Luna, I bind you, Matteo!"

Since I don't know the demon's name, I used Matteo's. And it works! Matteo's body instantly falls limp, landing on the cushions beside me with a thud. His eyes are shut, and he doesn't move.

I'm breathing hard, and I think I bruised my shoulder when I fell, but I feel more alive than I have in years.

My magic.

It's *back*.

It courses through me like a thousand buzzing bees, like clouds filled with electricity before a thunderstorm. I laugh, because it feels so hexing good, and I've missed it like I'd miss air if I were drowning.

By Tierra, how have I lived like this for five years? A shadow of myself. A shell.

Diego is next to me, checking me over, and it takes a second before I can focus on what he's saying.

"Cat? Carajo, Cat, are you okay? What's going on? Are you hurt? Please talk to me, mi corazón."

I raise a hand to his cheek and brush my thumb over the line of blood there. I whisper, "Sana, sana, colita de rana." A healing rhyme for children. But there's a spark of magic between our skin as his cut heals.

"I'm okay, Diego." My voice is steady.

"Thank Sol." He pulls me into his arms for a fierce hug. With my shields wide open, I can feel his power too. There's so much of it. He's always been strong, but it's more refined now. He's honed it from the blunt force it used to be when we were kids. And where it was once fueled by teenage insecurity, it's sharpened by adult confidence.

But that's not all. I feel his desire too. It stokes my own, and before I can think about the wisdom of it, I'm turning my face to his and kissing him.

With a groan, he drags me onto his lap and kisses me back. Deeply this time, with swipes of tongue and nipping teeth. My magic pulses in response to his and I pull back only to undo the buttons of his shirt.

45

"Your magic," he says, panting. "It's back?"

"Sure seems that way. Take off your clothes."

"Cat." He lets out a surprised laugh. "We're not done here yet."

"What? Oh, right. There's still a demon in your brother's sleeping body."

"That was a brilliant spell, by the way." There's pride shining in his voice, and I soak it in. "I wanted to blast the demon back to whatever hellhole it crawled out of, but my parents would be annoyed if I'd blown my brother's body to bits."

"What do we do with him?"

Before we can decide, the door bursts open and our siblings pile in, hooting and hollering, followed by the silent camera operators.

My sister Crystal raises an open bottle of expensive champagne like it's a sword and she's going to war. "We're crashing the party!"

Diego's younger brother Lorenzo pushes into the room behind her. His face lights up when he sees Matteo passed out on the bench, and he barks out a braying laugh. "Looks like someone already partied too hard!"

A waitress follows everyone in, and I set the borrowed headband and glasses on her tray with a hundred-dollar bill. "Can you return these to the coat check attendant?"

Diego stands and tugs me to my feet. "Let's go."

I glance back at Matteo's prone form. Crystal and Lorenzo are drawing dicks on his face with an eyeliner pencil. No one seems to notice the apron tied around his neck. "He'll be out for a good twelve hours, maybe more," I say.

"Perfect." Diego wraps an arm around my waist, holding me close enough that I can feel the evidence of how much he wants me. The heat in his eyes matches the fire surging through my veins. "Because you and I have unfinished business."

I grab the front of his shirt and give him a sultry smile. "Come on, brujo. Let's get wicked."

CHAPTER SIX

$\mathcal{W}$e're already tearing each other's clothes off by the time we return to the Vampire Suite.

Diego stops kissing me long enough to pull my shirt over my head. "This isn't just because of all the magic we raised."

I kick off my sandals and reach for the waistband of his pants. "Definitely not. But we do need to get it out of our systems. And sex is, like, really good for grounding energy."

"Right. We should be grounded before we face the demon again tomorrow."

"And before we have to deal with our families."

"Totally."

We hit the bed half-dressed. I'm still wearing a white mini skirt and my bra. Diego's pants are open and his shirt is unbuttoned. We're both barefoot.

My magic is still on high alert, but now, it's utterly focused on Diego. Sex magic isn't my thing, but with Diego, maybe it could *become* my thing. Our thing. I don't know anymore.

All I'm sure of is that I want him. And he wants me.

Even though the return of my magic is overwhelming, I can't bring myself to slip chains on it again. I'm too happy to have it back. If it weren't for Diego right now, for what's happening between us, I'd be a wreck.

But with every taste of his lips, every touch of his hands on my body, he grounds me. Little by little, I feel myself settling.

At the same time, my need for him only grows.

That need started when we were in the closet, trapped in the dark together, my senses full of him. The feel of him getting hard, and knowing it was because of me.

Ever since that moment, the thought of being with him like this has been on my mind. There's no going back to how things used to be. I want him too bad.

Rolling him onto his back, I straddle his hips. The move pushes up my skirt and I'm sure he can see my panties. I walk my fingers down his bare chest, heading for the intriguing bulge in his pants.

"You want me," I purr.

"Blessed Sol, Cat. I should think that's obvious." He sounds exasperated.

"Not just now. In the closet. And at dinner last night."

"Cat." His voice is serious. "He cups the back of my neck, drawing me down so our faces are inches apart. "I have *always* wanted you."

He kisses me hard, and all his feelings pour into me. Years of wanting me, adoring me, wishing he could find the words to tell me, to break us out of the cycle of rivalry we were locked in.

That *I'd* locked us in.

I'm still processing the depth of his feelings for me when he rolls me onto the mattress and unzips my skirt. I lift a hand and run it through his hair. "Diego. I didn't know."

"It's okay."

"Why didn't you say anything?"

His lips twist in a rueful smile. "I was scared. And I thought you hated me."

I push up onto my elbows, a move that shoves my boobs into

his face. He doesn't seem to mind. "I didn't *hate* you. I just wanted to win."

"And as long as I was one step ahead of you, you paid attention to me." He shrugs. "That was enough."

"But what about after we graduated?"

He glances away. "I knew my mom cost you the valedictorian spot. I didn't think you'd ever forgive me for that. I went away to school, and when I came back…"

I finish for him. "I was gone."

"But now you're here." There's relief in his voice as his hand reaches behind my back. "I'm going to take off your bra now."

I shiver in anticipation. "Please do."

A second later his mouth is on me, tonguing me, and I no longer care about anything else. Not our families. Not the wedding. Not even the demon. All I care about is his lips trailing kisses down my body, his hands tugging down my skirt and my panties.

All I care about is getting Diego just as naked as I am.

I fling my magic at him and his pants fly off, landing in a heap on the floor.

He lets out a husky laugh. "I was waiting to see if you'd do something like that."

"You're a tease."

I use my hands to pull his boxers down his hips, then let my magic whisk them away. We're both fully, gloriously naked, and I can't wait another minute to feel him against me. Throwing myself on him, we roll around on the black velvet bedspread, heat building between us as we touch and kiss. I'm already panting by the time his hand slides between my legs and I arch my hips, welcoming his fingers.

But it isn't enough to be touched. I need to touch him too. My hands explore his body, learning him. He's leanly muscled and tanned darker from the Miami sun, with neatly trimmed chest hair and multiple tattoos. Finally, I reach down and grasp the part of him that's made his interest in me clear since the broom closet.

His eyes roll back and he groans. "Sol preserve me, Cat. You're going to kill me."

"Oh no, you don't," I murmur. "I'm nowhere near done with you."

He kisses me, and our magic builds even higher as we urge each other on. The energy takes on a different quality, something edgy and needy, as we explore every inch of each other's bodies, bringing pleasure but delaying the ultimate climax.

When Diego breaks away from me and scoots to the edge of the bed, I feel bereft at the loss of his touch.

"Where are you going?" I ask, breathless with desperation.

"Condoms. They're in my bag on the bathroom counter."

"Allow me."

I twist my fingers in an exaggerated beckoning motion. A condom comes flying out of the bathroom. Diego snatches it in mid-air with his left hand.

His grin is devilish. "Neat trick."

"Lots more where that came from. Get over here so I can ride that broomstick all night."

He crawls toward me, snickering. "Baby, I'm going to stir your cauldron 'till it bubbles over."

I can't hold back my laughter. "I've missed witchy innuendo."

"Give me a second. I've got something about pointy hats on the tip of my tongue."

But I shake my head. "No more seconds, Diego. I need you."

He lowers himself over me. "You have me, Cat. I'm all yours."

I'm so ready for him, the first thrust is pure bliss. I dig my nails into his back as we move together, finding a rhythm that matches the magic pulsing around us, between us, within us. I don't know where his power ends and mine begins.

My toes curl against the black silk bedsheets as he drives me higher and higher. The connection is so strong, I can sense what he's feeling too, and it magnifies my own response. Pure passion, but also a deeper desire. Yes, he wanted this, but it's not all he wants from me. Normally, that would scare me a little, but I'm so in the moment with him, it just feels right. His name is on my lips, an incantation all its own. Yes, we are brujos. Yes, we have magic. But what's between us is a different kind of power, something I've never experienced before.

It's like the last piece of a puzzle has finally clicked into place. Utter satisfaction. Utter serenity.

Utterly orgasmic.

Diego gathers me against him and picks up the pace. I'm sweaty and so swamped with pleasure, I can barely keep track of my own limbs, but I manage to wrap them around him like vines. And then I cling to him for dear life as the climax builds. Within me, yes, but I can feel he's racing for it too.

I close my eyes, holding onto him with everything I have. He groans.

And then I let go.

Dual waves of pleasure and magic crash over me, his and mine. My mind goes blank. My body is pure sensation. I'm floating on a current of bliss, remnants of passion zipping through me like mini supernovas. My magic finally settles into something manageable, a contented purr of energy beneath my skin.

Diego gently lays me on the bed and brushes the hair out of my face.

"You okay?"

"Mmm. So much better than okay."

He's breathing hard and his eyelids droop like he's about to fall asleep, but he hovers a hand over my head, my heart, my belly. Taking a reading of me. "Seems like your magic has leveled out," he says.

"It has. Thank you." I pull his face down to mine for a light kiss.

The look in his eyes is almost wistful as he strokes my cheek. "I meant it, Cat. This wasn't just about the magic for me."

I lean into his touch. "I know."

With a last swipe of his thumb over my lips, he rolls off the bed and heads for the bathroom.

I watch him go, and I'm not offended when he shuts the door behind him. Truthfully, I need a minute too.

As much as I want to tell myself that this is just physical attraction, just grounding magic, it's more. I know Diego. And he knows me. He understands me in a way no one else does. Not my family. Not my friends and coworkers in New York. Not any of the guys I dated briefly, both here on Isla Bruja or when I was pretending to be a regular non-magical human working in the fashion industry.

I am argumentative and never satisfied. I am competitive as fuck. I'm stubborn. But I also work my butt off. I'm a kickass fashion designer. And I'm loyal. Brave. Loving.

Diego sees all of that in me. And being with him makes me remember who I used to be. Who I am. Who I wanted to be, before my magic left me.

Maybe I can be more than I've been, without pushing myself to be too much.

Maybe with a grounding force like Diego, I won't feel compelled to work myself into the ground to prove I'm better than my peers, better than my sisters, better than anyone on the island thought someone from my family could be.

But we have bigger problems right now. Our first two attempts to rid Matteo of the demon have failed. We only have one more chance before the wedding, and now the demon knows we're onto him.

And I still have to enchant my sister's dress.

Good thing my magic is back!

Diego finishes up and I take my turn in the bathroom. Now that the excess magic has been grounded, I'm exhausted by the events of the night. By our brush with death. By my revelations about Diego. By the return of my magic and an out-of-this-world orgasm.

He's in the center of the bed when I return, and he holds out his arms for me to join him. I climb onto the bed and cuddle up beside him. It shouldn't feel so right, but it does. More right than sleeping on opposite sides with miles of empty mattress between us.

He kisses my forehead and snuggles us into the pile of pillows. The air in the room is cool and smells like lilies and old, damp stones. It's a bit like sleeping in a mausoleum, if I'm being honest. But as long as Diego's arms are around me, I don't care where we are.

CHAPTER SEVEN

To my delight and my mother's dismay, Caro picked black as the color scheme for her wedding. Part of me suspects Caro did this for the express purpose of annoying our mom, because while Caro is the Good Daughter who will go along with something like a marriage merger, she is also the Queen of Passive Aggression.

Across from me, Diego taps his chin in thought. "I'm gonna... finger you like a ouija board."

I snort at Diego's latest attempt at brujería dirty talk. He's keeping me company while I enchant Caro's enormous black wedding dress in our room at the inn. We're supposed to be finalizing our plan to banish the demon, but we're also flirting. "That's a reach."

"I'm running out of ideas. Your turn."

I chew my lip as I think. "Hmm. I'm gonna...lick your magic wand!"

He nods approvingly. "Good one. Let's see. I'm going to, uh... make your pussy...my familiar?"

"Madre del Mar, Diego. That's terrible."

"I know. I'm sorry. Just be glad I didn't make it a play on your name."

"If you ever call me Pussycat, I'm hexing you."

"And I would deserve it."

That morning, before picking up Caro's dress, we swung by La Casa de Paz to check on Matteo after the binding spell wore off. Diego had theorized that the influx of wedding guests was spreading the camera spell thin. Sure enough, Matteo had seemed seriously hungover, weakened but unafraid, if his murderous glower was anything to go by.

While the other Paz brothers took Matteo to Miami for a fresh shave, Diego had stayed behind to work out a plan with me.

He's quiet for a long minute. "How does it feel?"

For a second I think he's talking about our mind-blowing sex the night before, but then he gestures at the wedding dress.

"It's been a while since you've done this."

"It has." My hands caress the voluminous skirt, layering in enchantments pulled from the air itself. Unlike ritualistic magic, I don't use many tools for fabric alchemy. Just the garment, the elements, and my own power.

I mull over his question. Despite the inflow of magic last night, I feel clumsy and out of practice. I keep negating the enchantments and starting over.

Yet even with the difficulties, working on this dress feels more like coming home than returning to Casa Cartagena did. I *missed* this. I missed creating for the sake of creating, not for money, or power, or fame, but because I enjoyed the satisfaction of channeling the elements through my body into a beautiful design.

And I can no longer ignore how every garment I created in New York felt incomplete. How *I* felt incomplete.

Finally, I have an answer for Diego. "It feels right."

He smiles and brushes a hand over my hair, hanging loose down my back. "Yo entiendo."

"You use a similar process in your cooking, right?"

"Sort of. When I went to culinary school, I liked it, but it felt like something was missing. So I developed a precise procedure for my recipes, something the chefs can replicate. And of course, I layer spells on all the kitchen supplies."

"You're a genius. I can't wait to visit the restaurant."

"I can't wait to show it to you," he says fondly.

The enchantment I'm weaving into the lace stalls, and I wave my hands to dissipate it before starting over. I swallow hard, then meet his eyes. "I'm sorry I was so focused on beating you in school."

Diego shrugs like it's no big deal and returns to his seat in the armchair. "It's the only way you would have noticed me. You were so out of my league in all other ways. Besides, you made me better. My brothers used to tease me, but I never would have done so well if I weren't trying to keep up with you."

"You mean surpass me."

He shakes his head. "I didn't care about winning. You always deserved to be valedictorian, and part of me will never forgive my mother for sabotaging you. I just wanted to be with you wherever you were, and if that was at the top, I decided I'd do whatever it took to get there too."

"What would you have done if I'd been a mediocre student?"

"Probably found other ways to embarrass myself for your attention."

I laugh, but a more serious question occurs to me. "What made you leave Isla Bruja?"

He snorts. "Have you met my mother?"

"Fair point. So why stay so close?"

"I missed it. Not enough to move back into my parents' house after college, but enough to settle down in Miami."

My fingers trail over lace as I ponder his words. Diego knows what this world is like. He's found a way to make peace with it, a way to be himself and still have a relationship with his family on his own terms.

Maybe he can teach me how.

"Are you going back to New York after this?" His tone is hesitant.

"I don't know anymore," I murmur. "When I got here, I had every intention of leaving after the wedding was done. But now, I don't know."

"Why?"

I shift my shoulders, the conversation making me feel restless. "I went to New York to hide. To heal from burnout. But it took coming back to Isla Bruja to begin healing. And I think I'm done hiding."

"Because your magic is back?"

"Actually, I don't think it ever really went away."

"No?"

I touch my chest. "It was protecting me."

"How so?" He sounds genuinely curious.

"You know, the very first time I enchanted an outfit, it was for Caro to wear to a school dance. I did it because it was fun, a challenging way to stretch my powers."

"I remember. You have an incredible skill, Cat."

"Thanks. But the attention she got flowed over onto me, and I threw myself into designing more looks for my mom and my sisters. The orders came pouring in."

"It's a heady feeling. Hard to give up."

"It was." I'd reveled in it. Until the cost became too high.

"In school, I was focused on being number one," I explain. "But after we graduated, I needed a new goal. I was already seeing my family's status rise through my design work, so that became my focus. To help my family get to the top."

He nods. "I understand the impulse. Our society is all about family reputation and collective power."

"Exactly. It became like an obsession. With every creation, I was trying to outdo the one I'd made before. It wasn't healthy, though. And I think my magic cut me off to protect me, to force me to reevaluate what's truly important."

"And what's that?"

"Me. My own health and happiness. I felt a lot of pressure, and while some came from my family and some from the people speculating about what I'd come up with next, a lot of that pressure came from me."

"Why do you think that was?"

"It doesn't take a rocket scientist to figure it out. I just...never felt good enough. I thought, if I could be the best at what I did, then I could finally relax. But how could I do that when I kept moving the goal posts?"

"Cat." He holds my gaze with those soulful brown eyes. "Please believe me when I say you are and have always been enough."

"I...I think I'm starting to realize that now. It's going to take more time to sink in, though."

"Take all the time you need. It took me a while to figure out how to have both, to do what I wanted, but still navigate my place within my family."

"It helps to know you've done it."

"We can work on it together." He's quiet for a moment. "And New York? I'll be honest, I've been following your career and it doesn't look like you slowed down."

"I didn't. It's hard to admit that, but I just found a new area to excel in. So what if I didn't have my magic? I'd find my place in the human fashion industry and do my best to reach the top there." I pause and shake my head. "I went there to heal, but I never stopped working. I was still hiding. From myself. You know, these last few days have been the longest vacation I've had in two years."

"I don't know that I'd call this a vacation," he says, his tone wry. "But if you let me, I'll show you what a real vacation is like."

I smile, imagining what it would be like to travel with him. "Mmm. I think I'd like that."

"You're not the only one with a tendency to throw yourself into your work, you know. But when you opened that closet door and I saw you again, I got the feeling that now was the right time for us, if only I had the courage to tell you."

I look over at him with affection. "You've changed a lot."

He shrugs. "Not so much. I've just learned not to let fear get in the way."

"Have I been doing that?"

"Only you can answer that question, mi corazón."

Before I can reply, the enchantments finally start to take hold in the wedding dress, and I'm flooded with immense satisfaction. Is there any better feeling than creating something from nothing using your own two hands?

I get caught up in the work, and we discuss our final attempt to rid Matteo of the demon.

The plan is to perform a good old-fashioned exorcism. It is, unfortunately, not something either of us has much experience with. I assisted my mother with a few when I was younger, but Caro was always better at it than I was.

Alas, Caro is fully under the demon's spell, and she's turned into even more of a bridezilla than I expected she'd be for a wedding she doesn't care about. I've lost count of the number of times she's screamed, "Everything has to be *perfect!*" at someone or something. The last time she said it, it was to a potted plant. The poor thing's leaves shivered in fear.

Diego is flipping through one of Nestor's spell books when I sit back and let out a long sigh.

"There. It's done."

He sets the book aside and comes up behind me to look at the dress.

"It's a masterpiece, Cat. Everyone's going to want to hire you again after this."

I exhale, then let out a moan when his hands knead the sore muscles at the base of my neck. "They'll have to take a number," I say.

"Do you think you'll open for business again, now that your magic's returned?"

"I'll figure it out later. For now, we have a demon to banish."

The ceremony's not scheduled until evening, and the only hitch in our plan to stick together is that we'll have to split up to get dressed with our respective wedding parties. Aside from the danger, it'll also be the most time we've spent apart from each other since we returned to Isla Bruja, and I've already gotten used to having Diego near.

I turn in his arms and kiss him, because I want to and I can.

He kisses me back, and before I know it, my panties are gone and I'm unzipping his shorts.

He breaks the kiss to ask breathlessly, "Are we really going to be this much of a cliche?"

"You mean the maid of honor and best man having a quickie before the wedding?"

"Yeah."

"I'm okay with it if you are."

"I am," he growls.

"Then let's do it."

I kneel on the fainting couch. Behind me, Diego pushes my dress up to my waist and shoves his shorts down to mid-thigh. He has condoms in his pocket.

Two dress forms stands sentinel at the other end of the room, modeling Caro's gown and my bridesmaid dress. It feels like they're watching us, so I extend a hand and make a twirling motion with my finger. The headless displays spin around to face the wall.

There, that's better.

I give myself over to the moment, to Diego. To the feel of him driving into me. To the connection between our magics.

We're both alchemists, after all. I work with fabric and he works with food, but it's the same process. Our magic has always understood each other, even when we didn't.

Our climax is quick and explosive, and does a lot to calm me down.

I give him a sleepy smile over my shoulder. "Thanks for that."

"Anytime." He presses a kiss to my spine, then lowers my dress.

When I stand, my knees wobble a little, and he steadies me with an arm around my waist. I cup his cheek with my hand, and he leans in.

"Be careful today." He murmurs the words against my lips.

"You too."

"I mean it. I'll be lost if something happens to you."

"I know. You need me for the spell."

"Cat." His voice deepens. "I need you for more."

His serious expression scares me a little, but instead of brushing him off or making a joke, I embrace the tension and say what's on my mind. "Diego, I...I want more too."

The strain around his eyes eases, and he nods. "Good."

Before he leaves for La Casa de Paz, we layer every kind of protection charm we can think of on ourselves to keep us from falling under the cameras' spell. And then there's nothing left to do.

After one last kiss, Diego's gone.

I miss him already.

CHAPTER EIGHT

*I*t's showtime. Since Caro's dress is finished, I shower and do my makeup, then put on my bridesmaid dress. My dress is black and lacy with skinny straps and a plunging neckline. I'm a little sad Diego won't get to see me in it until the ceremony, because I look *hot*. Once my hair is secured in a low bun, I teleport to Casa Cartagena to fulfill my Maid of Honor duties and help my sister prepare for her big day.

Casita has converted one of the spare bedrooms into a bridal suite, and I'm packed in with my four sisters, my mom, and my grandma. Three generations of brujas in one place, and even though most of them are caught in the demon's spell, it's still pandemonium.

Abuela pulls me aside and pats my hand. I feel a flare of protective magic from her. "Ay, qué bueno. You look so relaxed, my dear."

I am sure she can tell that Diego and I just had sex, and if she didn't already know, my blush gives it away. "Just looking forward to the ceremony."

Her dark eyes sharpen. "You'll make sure it goes well, sí?"

I nod. "I will, Abuela."

She looks over at my mother, who is making a show of primping in the mirror for the cameras. With a deep sigh, my grandmother shakes her head and goes to check on my youngest sister, Corinne.

I'm a bundle of nerves by the time we all troop downstairs to meet the Paz boys. Diego, his two younger brothers, and a cousin make up Matteo's groomsmen. Matteo looks alert, but strained, as relatives pepper him with their opinions about the wedding. I thank Luna for the distraction.

Diego appears at my side, and I am truly unprepared for the sight of him in a tux. It accentuates his long lean lines and the breadth of his shoulders. His hair is styled back and he looks like a model.

I give him an appreciative once-over. "Hey nerd. You clean up pretty good."

"Not so bad yourself, Salutatorian."

He says it fondly, like it's an inside joke between the two of us. Over the last few days, the word has lost its sting. That, plus the sharp look in his eye, lets me know he's still himself.

I grab his lapels and pull him in for a kiss. "You're *my* valedictorian, got it?"

His hand settles into the curve of my neck, and he strokes his thumb over my pulse point. "It was only ever for you, mi corazón."

Knowing that our rivalry was one-sided, that he was just trying to be close to me however I'd let him, is bittersweet. What else did I misinterpret back then?

But we're here now. We're older, wiser, and hotter. I don't know what the future holds for us, but I'm hoping it includes making up for lost time.

If we survive this wedding.

The ceremony is going to be held outside on the lawn, leading out to the water. A short, raised pier has been added, with an arbor draped in black tulle and adorned with blush pink and bordeaux colored roses. Overhead, la Luna rises high and full, blessing us all. It's almost time.

Rows of chairs fill the lawn, occupied by immediate and extended family members, close friends, Isla Bruja council members, and high witches from around the world. It's a brujería who's who, and even more people will be showing up for the reception.

The cameras are everywhere, and I can't tell who's already in a trance or not. I stick to the plan, avoiding the cameras as I chat with guests, and using the "I think I hear my mother calling" excuse whenever I see a camera approaching.

I also play that card anytime someone makes a snide comment about how I abandoned my customers.

Gee, so sorry I burned out and cost you all the opportunity to wear "a Catalina original" to my own sister's wedding. It's everything I can do not to roll my eyes right in their faces.

"I think I hear my mother calling," I tell a young woman and her wife. We're related somehow, but I can't remember if it's through my mom or my dad. I slip into the crowd and find my way back to Diego's side. We're cutting it close, waiting to do the exorcism during the ceremony, but it's the only time we can be sure we'll have everything we need. And, we hope, the demon will be too distracted to stop us.

Finally, the music begins, and the wedding party assembles on the patio to pair off.

Diego cocks his head and listens for a moment, his dark eyebrows drawing together in confusion. "Is that what I think it is?"

I smother a snicker. "A string version of 'Take Me to Church'? Yeah. It's part of Caro's subtle revenge on our mother."

"Truly diabolical."

I check in with Sophie the flower girl, crouching down to her height. She's my cousin's daughter and cute as a button with her round brown cheeks and springy ringlets. She's also barely four, so I'm a little worried about the role she's playing in our exorcism.

"Are you excited to be the flower girl, Sophie?"

"Oh yes. So excited!"

"Do you remember what you have to do for the wedding?"

"I have a basket and there's flower petals in it. They're red, pink, red, red…"

She continues naming the colors of each individual petal. I straighten with a sigh and take Diego's arm.

Sophie's basket isn't only holding rose petals. It's hiding a bag of salt I'll need to cast a circle around the demon.

The song changes to a string version of 'Despacito.' Beside me, Diego is practically shaking with suppressed laughter.

"Matteo hates this song," he mutters.

"I bet you a million dollars that's why Caro chose it."

"There's no way I'm taking that bet."

"Smart man."

It feels good to be able to laugh and joke at a time like this. Otherwise, I'll focus too much on the way my stomach is tied up in knots.

I'll focus too much on the abject terror.

I look out at the assembled guests. Many of them my relatives, all of them people I've known my whole life. I went to New York to get far away from all this, from the expectations and pressure of being a resident of Isla Bruja, a member of the magical Latinx diaspora in the States.

Now? I only want to protect them.

Sophie goes first, dropping her flower petals with deliberate motions. It's adorable, but when she reaches the pier, she does something I probably should've predicted, but didn't.

She tosses the mothereffing basket right into the water.

Diego sighs as Sophie's dad snatches her up before she jumps in the water too. "It's okay. We still have the candles."

Since the binding spell actually worked last night, and the

wedding theme is goth black, Diego went around carving tiny binding symbols into all the black candles.

Tierra bless Caro's dark sense of humor.

The wedding planner gives us our cue, and we walk down the aisle between the chairs, heading for the pier. Diego's mother waits there with El Libro de Brujería, the sacred text of Isla Bruja. As High Priestess and mother of the groom, she is serving as officiant for the ceremony. Diego's father is seated in the audience.

I'm still a little scared of Señora Paz, but it's clear she's in the demon's thrall. Her eyes are glazed, and she's staring off into space. Plus, I haven't heard her make a critical remark about me or my sisters all night.

Matteo stands in front of her. He makes eye contact with me and sends me a smug grin.

The demon inside him is awake and well, and he has no fear of me.

Diego pats the hand I have wrapped around his bicep, and I realize I must be squeezing him. I try to loosen my grip and instead send up a silent protection prayer while strangling the hex out of my bouquet of black roses.

En el nombre del Sol, la Luna, la Tierra, el Mar, y el Espíritu, protegeme.

Diego and I part at the pier and take our places on either side of the arbor. Without him, I feel exposed and alone, barely three feet from the demon.

The others join us, and then my father walks Caro down the aisle.

I'm proud of her dress. It's not my best work, or even my most outrageous. But it's perfect for Caro.

It's nearly a living thing, capturing all her dark and twisted visions for this wedding.

The bodice fits her perfectly, giving her all the lift and cleavage she demanded. We inherited our mother's boobs, and they are, inarguably, our best assets.

Caro's arms are encased in lace. The patterns move like living tattoos, changing from flowers to snakes to skulls, and back again.

The full skirt billows like it's made of thick, black smoke, giving the appearance that she's walking on fog. Behind her, the ends of her veil curl and flutter like ink in water.

The guests gasp as she arrives. She walks with her eyes downcast, her false lashes dark against her tan cheeks. Her lipstick is wine red to match her bouquet, a thing of beauty all its own with roses, trailing vines, and gold-tipped leaves. It weighs a ton.

Caro reaches us on the pier. Dad takes his seat next to Mom, who is wearing a long white mermaid gown because, as she put it, "Someone should be wearing white at this wedding."

I glance up at the moon. *Luna, please give me strength.*

Señora Paz opens the ceremony. "Dearly beloved, we are gathered here today—"

To witness an exorcism.

"—to join esto brujo y esta bruja in magical matrimony."

In a wedding of the damned.

I pay close enough attention for my cue, but I am otherwise completely absorbed in not hyperventilating. Finally, Señora Paz closes El Libro de Brujería and begins the vows.

"Mijo, repeat after me. I, Matteo Alejandro Paz De León…"

Diego and I wait for the exact moment the demon opens Matteo's mouth to speak the vows. And then we burst into action.

Using my telekinetic power, I grab El Libro and hurl it into Diego's waiting hands. At the same time, all the candles surrounding the assembled guests flare like torches, including the single additional candle Diego hid among the arbor. The binding symbols glow with golden light.

With the circle cast, I turn my magic toward holding Matteo's body immobile. Maybe I can't banish the demon, but I can affect Matteo's carbon-based form. It's difficult as all hex, and I feel the demon fighting to move. Matteo's eyes glow red and his perfect teeth bare in a snarl.

With the book in one hand and a black candle in the other, Diego begins the exorcism. "By the light of el Sol, I command you."

The demon roars. My arms shake from the effort of holding him still.

"By the shadow of la Luna, I command you."

Matteo's fists clench and his muscles bulge. I wouldn't be surprised if he rips the seams of his suit jacket like he's the Hulk. My power, so newly returned, struggles to contain him. Tears prick the corners of my eyes and my knees wobble.

"By the soul of el Mar, I command you."

"Diego!" His name is torn from my throat as I feel my hold on Matteo slipping. "I'm losing him!"

"Looking for this, mi sirenita?"

I turn my head at the familiar voice and spot El Capitán standing at the edge of the pier. He's holding Sophie's flower basket.

"Yes," I say breathlessly. "Gracias al Mar, yes!"

Cap sets the basket on the pier, gives me a salute, then backflips into the water without a splash.

Diego continues the incantation. "By the heart of la Tierra, I command you."

Matteo's upper body strains. Diego meets my eyes and moves further away from his brother. At Diego's nod, I release the demon and send all my power to the bag of salt hidden in the basket. Matteo lurches forward, arms outstretched, ready to strangle Diego before he can complete the ritual.

But I am starting to love my former rival, and I'll be damned if I lose him now.

The full force of my power snaps back to me. I reach a hand in the direction of the basket, using my magic to tear into the bag. The salt is, miraculously, not even a little damp.

Throwing my other arm toward Matteo, the grains of salt fly through the air in a barely visible streak of white. Just before the demon reaches Diego, the salt connects in a floating circle, encasing Matteo's waist like one of Saturn's rings.

His body lurches to a stop and there's murder in his eyes, but we have him now.

Diego invokes the final deity. "By the will of el Espíritu, I command you—release my brother's body at once!"

At the word "release," there's a pulse in the air, and the demon's spell is broken. One second, everyone is watching the proceedings with mild surprise. The next, they're screaming. All around, the camera operators turn translucent, like ghosts.

My mother takes one look at what's going on and leaps to her feet. She sprints down the pier on her spindly heels and snatches the book from Diego. Her eyes go full black as she advances on the demon, and the expression on her face chills me to the bone. I haven't seen her look like this since Crystal set the school gym on fire.

Mom is about to exorcise the shit out of this demon.

"*How. Dare. You.*" She plants a hand on Matteo's chest, fingers splayed. Thin tendrils of smoke rise from beneath her palm and she bares her teeth in rage. "*How dare you attack my family, you comemierda?*"

The demon screams in Matteo's throat, and Mom spares me a reassuring black-eyed glance.

"Good job, honey. I'll take it from here."

I release my telekinetic hold on the salt and stagger backward. Diego is there to catch me. His mother joins mine, chanting the ritual prayers of la Luna to purify her son and bring him back to his own body. Magic is all about balance, and they work together, my mother pushing the demon out, High Priestess Paz calling her son's consciousness back in.

Abuela joins us, eyeing the protective way Diego holds me. She sends me a sly smile.

"A-*ha*! I knew it wasn't all an act."

"Abuela, were you ever under the demon's spell?"

She scoffs. "¿Yo? Claro que no."

I gape at her. "Then why didn't you tell me?"

"Porque I knew you two could handle it. And if you couldn't, I was prepared." Abuela pulls a long, wicked-looking knife out of her tiny purse, like some kind of octogenarian assassin Mary Poppins. "Did you think I'd let a demon marry my granddaughter? Besides, you and Diego were getting along so well."

I pinch the bridge of my nose. "Abuela, in the future, exorcism is *not* a good matchmaking device."

"Pero it worked, sí?" She winks and moves to Caro, who has thrown her massive bouquet into the water.

"It's a sign from la Luna," Caro declares. "I'm not marrying Matteo."

Matteo, who is still undergoing an exorcism by two Boricua mamis, has nothing to say on the matter.

My youngest sister Corinne giggles with glee as she films the proceedings on her phone. "This is un escándalo for the ages. I can't wait to upload it to InstaBruja."

Dad snatches the phone out of her hands. "No going viral at the expense of your sisters."

"Pero Daddy!"

"You know the rules."

My sister Cleo looks bereft. "Wait, you mean the cameras weren't real? ¡Coño!" She stomps off toward the house in tears.

Crystal snaps her fingers in Diego's face to get his attention. "Hey brujo. How about releasing the binding circle so we can all go inside and get drunk?"

"Oh right." Diego lets go of me and claps his hands. "The circle is closed."

The clap reverberates through the space and the guests cheer.

Crystal whistles to get their attention. "Open bar, baby! Last one to the ballroom's a pendeja!"

Most of the crowd moves to follow her. Some gather around

the pier calling out advice to my mother and Señora Paz, but more than a few people cast speculative looks in my direction.

Diego's great-aunt winks at us. "Ay, pero maybe we can have a wedding today after all?"

Another vieja—possibly a cousin of my dad's—checks her watch. "If they hurry up with the exorcism we can fit in another ceremony before la Luna sets."

I cover my face and mumble to Diego through my fingers. "Get us out of here."

"This is your land, remember? I can't teleport in or out. But you can."

"Blessed Luna. That's right, I can!"

I throw my arms around him and call my magic, directing it to take us to the inn. Wind rushes around us and a second later, I'm standing on asphalt instead of grass. Nestor is sweeping the front walk when we appear.

"Welcome back, nenes!" he calls. "Did you banish el demonio?"

Diego rubs his forehead. "You knew about that too?"

"Claro que sí. Matteo was never so interesting as he was this week. That's why I didn't go."

I kiss Nestor's cheek on our way into The Crone's Nest. "Thank you, Nestor. For everything."

He winks at me from beneath the magenta bangs of his wig and continues sweeping. Before we can close the front door behind us, he calls out, "Don't forget to return all my supplies to where they belong!"

Diego shakes his head and sighs as we climb the stairs to our room. "Everyone really does know everything about each other on Isla Bruja."

"I wouldn't be surprised if your tío and my abuela were in cahoots."

"I'm *sure* they are."

Inside our room, I snap my fingers and all the candles flare to life, a small act of magic I'll never take for granted again. "We make a pretty good team, don't we?"

"I can't think of anyone I'd rather exorcise a demon with."

I set my phone on the dresser and bend down to remove my heels. "We should get out of these clothes."

"Not yet." Diego pulls out his phone and holds it with the screen facing us. "Let's take a selfie."

"Oh right. We were supposed to take photos after the ceremony. I guess that's not happening, huh?"

"Not likely. I can't imagine Matteo is going to want to remember this night."

I slip my arms around Diego's waist and smile for the camera. He snaps a few pictures, including one where he's kissing my temple. My smile is big and genuine, and even though my eyes are half-closed, it's my favorite one.

"Text me those," I tell him.

"I will. I didn't get to tell you earlier, but you look stunning."

"Thank you. So do you. Handsome, I mean." I touch his nose ring gently. "I like this."

"I'm glad."

I lower my hand and place it over his heart. "I like this too."

He tosses his phone onto the bed and slides his arms around me. "What's next for us, Cat?"

I rest my head on his chest, relishing the solid, steady feel of him. I don't need a crystal ball to know our outlook looks good. "What's next? I think…"

My stomach rumbles, and I laugh. "I think you need to make me dinner."

Diego grins. "With pleasure."

CHAPTER NINE

*S*ince we skipped the reception, Diego asks Nestor if he can use the B&B kitchen to cook for me. Nestor agrees, on the condition that we leave him leftovers.

Diego makes Puerto Rican food with a gastropub twist, using magic to speed some of the steps along. After settling in at the counter, I ask him about the restaurant, and he fills me in on his life since I last saw him.

It's a joy to watch Diego bustle around the kitchen with efficient and, if I'm being honest, sexy movements. His confidence is on full display here. He is master of his domain.

This is who Diego really is. Dedicated, ambitious, and focused on honing his craft. He works hard, but he's not competitive like I am. Still, it's nice to know he doesn't mind that part of me.

It's time I let go of my annoyance over the valedictorian thing. Diego himself is a bigger prize than any trophy or certificate.

As I nibble on yuca fries dipped in cilantro aioli, I remember Diego's comment from earlier in the day, about not letting fear get in the way of what he wants. Is that what I've been doing? Before, I wouldn't have said so. I always went after what I wanted with single minded determination, like the valedictorian spot, or elevating my family through my magical couture business, or even being a world-famous luxury fashion designer.

But were those things *really* what I wanted? Why had I gone after them? What had I thought they'd bring me?

I think back to that first dress I enchanted for Caro, and it hits me. I am one of five daughters in a narcissistic family. My over-achieving started as a way to stand out. To receive praise. But making clothes also brought me love and attention. From my parents. From my sisters. From my peers and the elders in the Isla Bruja community.

Love and attention. That's what I've been after all this time.

And here's a man who cares about me not *because* of my accomplishments, but in spite of my drive to attain them.

I set down my fork. "Diego? Do you care if I never enchant another garment?"

He looks over from the stove with a puzzled expression and shakes his head. "I just want you to be happy. If it makes you happy to design clothes, do it. But if it doesn't, then don't."

He makes it sound so simple. And, maybe it is.

"I think I'm going to get a place in Miami," I announce.

Diego nearly drops the pan he's holding. "You're what?"

"Remember what you said about being *close, but not too close?*" When he nods, I continue. "Reconnecting with my magic, with my family, with *you*…I've felt more fulfilled in these last few days than I have since I left. I think I'm ready to come back."

Diego washes his hands quickly, then comes over to kiss me.

"What's that for?" I ask, surprised.

"I thought getting you to move down here was going to take a lot more persuasion on my part. It didn't occur to me that all I had to do was feed you."

I toss a wadded up napkin at him. "It's not just the food. New York never really felt like home. Only…"

"What?"

I swallow hard. "What if it happens again? The burnout, I mean. What if it's permanent next time?"

Diego hugs me to him and gently strokes my hair. "It won't happen, mi corazón. You're a different person now, and if you do start up your business again, it'll be for you, not your family."

"And I'll have you to make sure I take breaks."

"Hey, if anyone knows your overachiever patterns, it's me."

He returns to the stove, and I resume snacking. He's right. Things are different now. And I'm finally realizing that my worth isn't tied to my achievements.

Diego whips up mofongo sliders and bacalao guisado over quinoa con gandules, along with a pitcher of piña coladas. Everything is the best thing I've ever tasted. The man truly has a gift.

Crystal calls just after we're done eating, and I can tell she's drunk.

"Yo sis. Guess what?" she slurs.

"Um, you're drunk?"

Crystal giggles. "No shit. That's too easy. Nah, it's something else."

I close my eyes. "Fucking hex, what else could it be?"

"*Caro* summoned the demon."

I nearly drop the phone. "Caro *what?*"

Diego's looking at me with concern, so I turn on speakerphone.

"Yeah," Crys continues. "Caro decided she couldn't go through with marrying Matteo because he quote-unquote *hates good music,* so she tried to summon the ghost of Mama Isabella to help her stop the wedding. But instead of our great-grandmother, she called a motherfucking demon instead!"

I glare at Diego, who is covering his mouth and shaking with laughter. "This is not funny," I hiss at him.

He wipes a tear from his eye. "Come on, it kind of is."

To Crystal, I say, "All this because Caro's too passive aggressive to tell Mom she changed her mind."

"Nailed it in one."

"And what about the camera operators?" I ask.

"Creepy shit. They were lost souls, but Mom helped them cross over. Anyway, there's a bottle of vintage Dom Perignon with my name on it. Toodles, witch! Have fun burning on your boyfriend's stake!"

She ends the call and I purse my lips in thought, mulling over the innuendo. "Okay, that one actually wasn't that bad."

Diego tilts his hand in the air, like *mas o menos*. "I wouldn't call it *good*, though."

I put my phone back in my pocket. "A demon. Wow. I didn't think Caro had it in her."

"She didn't. The demon was inside Matteo." He makes a sound like a cymbal crash—*badum-tiss*.

"She must really not have wanted to marry him."

"I can't blame her. Matteo's my brother and I love him, but he's a pendejo."

"You know the families are going to look to us next."

"It's in their nature."

"Don't be surprised if they plan us a wedding for next week using all of Caro and Matteo's leftover stuff."

"I'm sure my mom is already working on a spell to change the first names on the invitations to 'Cat and Diego.'"

I cover my face with my hands and groan at the thought of it. "What am I thinking, coming back to Florida? They're going to suck me back into family drama the second I sign a lease."

"We'll manage it together. It can't be any worse than exorcising a demon out of my brother."

"Don't tempt fate, Diego," I warn.

"All I'm saying is we can be adults with healthy boundaries."

"Still…how about we keep this quiet for now? Me moving to Miami, I mean. I want to explore what's happening between us without expectations or pressure. Let this be our own for a while."

"And Tío Nestor's."

I turn to see Nestor peeking around the edge of the door-frame. He waves.

"Nestor, can you keep a secret?" I call over to him.

"Oh, of course, of course, mi nenita. You know me. I don't say nothing to nobody." Nestor mimes locking his mouth with a key and tossing it over his shoulder.

That's a damn lie, but I don't call him on it. Instead, I take Diego's hand and lace our fingers together. "We'll tell them when we're ready."

"When *you're* ready. We've always been on your timeline, Cat."

I open my shields to his emotions and realize that's true. He's always been ready for me.

He lifts our joined hands and kisses my knuckles. "You know what happened when you found me in that broom closet?" he asks.

"No, what?"

The corner of his mouth twitches. "You swept me off my feet."

I'm still laughing when he kisses me.

EPILOGUE

Four months later

In a stunning turn of events, my sister Crystal elopes with Diego's brother Lorenzo. Apparently they hooked up after the wedding-turned-exorcism, and managed to keep their romance under wraps better than Diego and I did.

Our mothers are despondent at the missed opportunity to host another "wedding of the century." But like a good brother, Diego steps in and throws Crystal and Lorenzo a reception at his Miami restaurant. Since the moms finally got the merger they wanted, I announce that I've moved in with Diego.

My mother is ecstatic. "Honey, I'm so glad to have you closer. New York was just too far away. We missed you."

Diego's mother has a mercenary look in her eye. "Does this mean you're open for business again? I could use a new gown for the Temple gala next month."

Diego grits his teeth. "Mami, we talked about this."

I pat his arm. "It's okay, D. I'm thinking about it, Señora Paz."

"Call me Josefina. We're family now."

I incline my head. "When I'm open for business again, you'll be the first to know, Josefina."

Her smile is huge, and she does a little shimmy. "I have to tell the others."

Diego rubs my back. "The viejitas are going to be knocking down your door for appointments."

"Don't let my mother hear you calling her a viejita. She'll send a zombie after you. And I think you mean *your* door."

"*Our* door. And don't worry, I'll reinforce the warding spells."

"I knew there was a reason I kept you around."

He raises an eyebrow. "Only one reason?"

"Several reasons. A million reasons. Where do you want me to start?"

"Right here."

He kisses me, right there in front of everybody, and I don't even mind. Let the chismosas talk. I love him and he loves me.

And that's more than enough.

☾

DEAR READER

Thank you so much for picking up *What the Hex!* This short novella was first published as an audiobook for Audible Originals, and I'm thrilled that it's now available in ebook and print formats. Spending time—however brief—with these characters in Isla Bruja was a dream come true (the idea for the Cartagena family first came to me in 2015!) and I would love to explore this world even more. In fact, I already have an idea brewing (pun intended) for Cat's older sister Caro. So if you'd like to see more stories in this series, the best way to let me know is by leaving a review!

ACKNOWLEDGMENTS

Thank you so much for reading! This witchy novella started as an Audible Original audiobook, but before that, it was an idea that popped into my head many years earlier. When I received the opportunity to write a short paranormal rom-com, I was so excited to finally bring this story and these characters to life! It was a joy to write, and I hope it was a joy to read. *What the Hex* is truly a book of my heart and the kind of story I've been wanting to publish for a while, and I'm so grateful for the individuals who helped me make it happen!

As always, I must first thank my incredible agent Sarah E. Younger. When I was having paranormal rom-com FOMO, she encouraged me to dust off an idea I'd jotted down way back in 2015 and draft a proposal, which ended up becoming *What the Hex*! It was the perfect confluence of events, and I'm eternally grateful for Sarah's guidance through the process.

Huge thanks also go to my editor Allison Carroll and the team at Audible. They did a fantastic job and allowed me to tell this story and package it exactly how I wanted. It was a dream experience and one I'll never forget! And thank you to the rockstar team at NYLA for helping to convert this into the print and ebook editions. You have them to thank for the version you now hold in your hands.

Y muchas gracias to Mia and Jacqueline for joining this project and being so lovely and supportive of these characters! Jacqueline Grace Lopez, who narrated the audiobook, did a phenomenal job bringing this story to life with nuance, emotion, and humor. (If you haven't listened yet, the novella is free through Audible Plus!) María Dresden, the cover artist, is an absolute genius who perfectly gets my vision and always elevates it to the next level. Thank you both from the bottom of my heart!

Additional thanks to my publicist extraordinaire Kristin Dwyer—I'd be lost without you! And to the amazing community of writers I am lucky to be surrounded by: my Latinx Romance crew (Adriana Herrera, Angelina Lopez, Diana Muñoz Stewart, Liana De La Rosa, Mia Sosa, Natalie Caña, Priscilla Oliveras, Sabrina Sol, Zoraida Córdova, and more!), my Rebelles (including Evi Kline who helped me brainstorm), stellar romance writers Tracey Livesay and Nisha Sharma for keeping me company while I was drafting, and my coach Kate Brauning for keeping me on track!

And of course, I am grateful for my family, who understand when I disappear for weeks at a time to meet a deadline and love me anyway.

Last but certainly not least, I am so appreciative of all my readers! Thank you to everyone who listened to the audiobook and left such kind comments and reviews! I know it took me a while to get this book into another format, and I'm so grateful for your patience. If you're so inclined, I would love it if you left a review! I also hope to revisit this world and these characters again, so stay tuned and make sure you're subscribed to my newsletter. Thanks again!

KEEP READING FOR A BONUS WITCHY SHORT STORY FROM ALEXIS DARIA!

Two people dreaming of love find their wishes granted on the longest day of the year.

Emma Reyes has it bad for Logan Argento, the single dad next door. When he asks her to host his daughter's witch-themed birthday party, Emma leaps at the chance to help. She's been looking to shake up her usual Summer Solstice celebration, and this might be just what she needs. Because little does Logan know, Emma is a real witch pretending to be a regular person pretending to be a fake witch. Emma dreams of finding true love, but so far, her magical secret has made relationships impossible. Could Logan be the one to break her dry spell?

SOLSTICE DREAM

Chapter One

The Bruja Cove Herald
Weekly Horoscope
Pisces

This week, dear Pisces, you'll want to lean into your fluid, watery nature and go with the flow. Now is not the time to rigidly adhere to your usual routine. Stay flexible and keep an eye out for surprise opportunities. With Litha approaching, you'll want to embrace a mindset of abundance. Be clear about what you desire. You never know what dreams might come true!

"*W*hat time are you getting to the Midsummer Celebration this weekend?"

At the question, Emma Reyes looked up from the horoscope column in Bruja Cove's local newspaper. Her best friend—and technically her boss—Tatiana Lopez had joined her behind the counter at The Witch's Brew Café. Emma was on barista duty this sunny Monday morning while Tatiana unpacked the weekly shipment in the back.

"I'm not sure I'm going," Emma mused, folding *The Bruja Cove Herald* and setting it on a shelf under the counter.

"¿Por qué no?" Tatiana asked, her delicate eyebrows arching in surprise. "You had a great time last year."

"I did, but I think I want to do something different this year."

"Like what?"

Emma gave a little shrug. "I don't know. But according to my horoscope, the answer will come to me unexpectedly."

Tatiana gave her a bland look. "You know I write those horoscopes, right?"

"And they're never wrong." Emma shot her friend a sunny smile.

With a mock-bow, Tatiana went to the mini-fridge and topped off her iced coffee.

Emma perked up as a truck stopped in front of the café's big windows. "Another delivery," she said.

"I bet it's a t-shirt shipment." Tatiana gave her cup a swirl to mix the milk. "The new designs are due to arrive this week."

"I'll sign for it." Emma went to meet the delivery man at the door and returned to the counter with a large cardboard box that did indeed have the logo for their t-shirt printer on the label.

"Ooh, it's the 'Resting Witch Face' tees," Tatiana said, peeking into the box over Emma's shoulder. "Don't forget to take one."

"Thanks. I'll hang these up if you want to get back to inventory," Emma offered.

Tatiana slumped. "Don't remind me. I think I hear the many packages of biodegradable straws calling my name."

After Tatiana disappeared into the storage room, Emma unpacked the t-shirts and carried them to the small clothing rack in the front of the store. The café was quiet this morning, so she took her time folding some shirts artfully on a display table and putting the rest on hangers.

In addition to sustainably-sourced coffee, a selection of proprietary tea blends, and locally-made snacks, Witch's Brew sold witchy goodies like spell boxes—made by Emma—crystals, books, candles, and their top-selling item, witch-themed t-shirts. That day, Emma wore a tangerine-colored tee that said "Look What You Made Me Brew," while Tatiana sported a black tank that read "Big Witch Energy."

In Bruja Cove, California, such things were par for the course. Bruja Cove was a small coastal town in San Diego County that had long been a safe haven for the magically inclined. Non-witches lived there too, and if they were bothered by all the witchy stuff in plain sight, no one ever said so out loud. Locals jokingly called it the Salem of Southern California, minus the horrific history.

Emma had grown up in Philadelphia, part of a big Puerto Rican family. As much as she missed them, Philly had never felt like home, and Bruja Cove had called to her. After finishing college, she'd made the move. On her first day in town, she'd met Tatiana Lopez, proprietress of the Witch's Brew Café.

Tatiana was a green witch—highly skilled in herbal magic—who'd been born in the Dominican Republic. Tattoos of tropical flowers and plants covered her arms like sleeves, and she favored bold eye makeup. Tall and lithe, her brown skin seemed to glow with warm russet tones, and she kept her tight curls buzzed short and bleached blond.

Emma felt like she'd known the other witch forever, and they'd bonded instantly. Tatiana had needed help around the café, so Emma had started working there part-time, both as a barista and as a vendor. But when it came to magic, Emma still considered herself a solo practitioner.

Alas, she was solo in more ways than one.

She was down to the last three shirts when the wind chimes on the door jingled. Emma glanced over her shoulder as a man hurried inside.

Not just any man. It was Logan Argento, her hot next-door neighbor.

"Logan," she said, a little breathless. Her heart always beat faster at the sight of him. "How are you?"

Logan stopped short when he saw her, and his serious face broke into a wide grin. "Emma. I was hoping to find you here."

"Oh?" She gestured at the counter. "Did you want a coffee?"

"Yes, but…" He followed her and stood on the other side of the counter while she prepped his usual drink—dark roast with lots of two-percent milk, no sugar.

"But?" she prompted. He was watching her movements intently. The man was a mix of contradictions. He had a face made for deep brooding—dark heavy brows, piercing green eyes, a stern mouth, and a five o'clock shadow that covered his strong jaw at all hours of the day—but his smile was brilliant and infectious, like the sun breaking through clouds after a thunderstorm.

He snapped his gaze up to hers and his expressive brows dipped a little, as if in distress.

"I'm having a bit of an emergency," he said. "I heard you do kids' birthdays?"

"I do indeed. You're looking at Bruja Cove's answer to princess parties." Emma popped a compostable lid on the to-go cup. Logan always got his coffee to go, then stood around chatting with her for a bit. She wanted to believe it meant something, but maybe that was just wishful thinking, since they usually discussed mundane things like the differences in taste and texture of non-dairy milk substitutes.

"Any chance you're available this coming weekend?" A note of pleading entered the rich tones of his voice. "The face painter I hired for Kayla's eighth birthday had a family emergency and had to go out of town."

Emma slid the coffee over to him with a coy look. "I'm a bit offended you didn't ask me in the first place."

He raised an eyebrow. "If I'd known I lived next to a birthday party entertainer, I would have."

"You never asked," she said primly, accepting the five-dollar-bill he handed her. Logan and his daughter had moved to Bruja Cove in February, settling in the little American Craftsman-style bungalow next to Emma's own. "When is Kayla's party?"

"This Saturday."

A thrill of anticipation sparked inside her. "That's Litha. The summer solstice. The longest day."

Logan blinked. "Uh, yeah. I guess it is."

"I'll do it." This was what her horoscope had hinted at. A surprise opportunity to shake up her routine. Litha was a joyful day, all about abundance. What better way to spend it than with children, celebrating?

"You're a lifesaver!" The relief was evident in his voice and the way he slumped against the counter, bringing them closer together. "Let me know your fee, and whatever it is, I'll pay it."

"Will do." She passed him his change and, as usual, he dropped all of it in the jar labeled "Tip Your Local Witch."

"I can't thank you enough," he murmured in a low voice. With the emergency abated, his eyes met hers, and a simmering heat flared to life in their stunning depths. "I promise I'll make it up to you."

Emma bit her lip and his eyes flickered to her mouth. The way he turned on the sexy from one second to the next set her aflame. "You don't have to do that."

"But I want to." His gaze returned to hers. "Can I take you out for a drink sometime?"

This was it. He'd *finally* asked her out. They'd been playing this game for months. Whenever they chatted, he switched from light banter to smoldering glances at the drop of a pointed hat. She'd hoped it was only a matter of time before the embers ignited into a blaze.

She sucked in a shaky breath and nodded. "Uh-huh."

His grin flashed, hot and compelling. "Great. See you soon, neighbor."

He took the coffee and was gone, wind chimes tinkling in his wake.

Emma let out a long, slow breath. Logan Argento got her all twisted up inside. The flirty back-and-forth paired with those super-intense eyes made for an irresistible combo. It probably wasn't smart to get involved with the single dad next door, but she wanted to. *So* badly. It had been a long time since she'd dated anyone, and she could admit that she yearned for romantic companionship. Someone to cuddle, someone to eat breakfast with, someone to kiss goodnight. And more.

But she wasn't just a pretend witch for kids' birthday parties. She wasn't just a barista who assembled spell boxes of candles, herbs, and crystals. She didn't just celebrate the sabbaths with the other Bruja Cove residents in the park.

Emma was a witch—a *real* one. With elemental powers and a familiar and all. Her parents and grandparents, her aunts and uncles and cousins—all of them were witches. Emma had to be sure she could trust someone before telling them her secret. And so far, no one had come close. As much as she loved the idea of getting tangled up with Logan, in the long run, she was only looking at heartbreak.

With a sigh, she went back to hanging the last of the t-shirts.

CHAPTER TWO

"ARE YOU EXCITED FOR YOUR PARTY?"

Kayla looked up from her breakfast and tapped her chin, as if deeply considering Logan's question. "Yes," she finally replied and ate another spoonful of apple cinnamon oatmeal.

Logan patted her shoulder and went to the kitchen counter to stir milk into his coffee. Kayla had inherited his tendency to overthink things, although in looks, she took after her mother. Lisette, his ex-wife, was a metal-working artist who'd moved to Austin, Texas, after their divorce. Kayla had her corkscrew curls and smooth brown skin, but her dark eyebrows and pale green eyes were all Logan.

They'd only lived in Bruja Cove for a few months, after Logan had accepted a tenure-track political science professor position at UCSD and moved them down from San Francisco. He could've picked somewhere closer to the university campus, but the Bruja Cove school system was good and he'd liked the vibe of the town. Plus the house had been a steal, and in this housing market, he'd taken it as a sign that this move was meant to be.

Kayla had been slowly making some new friends, both at school and at the STEM-focused day camp she was enrolled in, but whenever he asked her if she wanted to schedule a playdate, she did the same finger-to-chin deep consideration before saying no. He hoped a lot of kids showed up today so he could observe her interactions with them on her home turf.

He'd checked out Emma's website after one of the camp counselors recommended her, and hadn't been surprised to see that the parties were witch-themed. Everything in Bruja Cove seemed to be, and the residents made the most of the name. Kayla loved all things Hotel Transylvania and Addams Family, so Logan figured this would be right up her alley.

Emma's website—"The Birthday Witch"—was full of pictures of small children running around dressed as witches. Everything was black, purple, and green, with an overabundance of spiders, cobwebs, and skulls. Snacks were served in mini cauldrons and drinks in child-sized goblets. Activities included science projects disguised as "magic"—baking soda and vinegar "potions," giant bubble "force fields," and a water-powered bottle rocket with a tiny witch attached to the side. She had games like "Pin the Spider on the Web" and something like musical chairs but with broomsticks. All the children got wands to take home as party favors, and goody bags shaped like brooms.

While Kayla might only be nominally excited for the party today, Logan, for one, was looking forward to it. Any chance he got to talk to Emma, he counted as a win for the day. She was always sweet to Kayla, fixed his coffee perfectly, and looked cute as hell puttering around her herb garden in funny t-shirts and tiny cut-off shorts. She was so freaking pretty, with dark hair that fell in shoulder-length waves, golden skin, and big, dark brown eyes. Her finely-arched brows and the little smile she always wore made her look like she knew a secret.

Whatever that secret was, he was dying to know. He'd been wanting to ask her out for months but kept talking himself out of it. Would it be presumptuous? Was she just being polite because they were neighbors and he frequented the coffee shop where she worked? He didn't think he misinterpreted the way she lit up when she saw him, but just in case he was, he didn't want to take advantage of the familiarity or make her uncomfortable. And he wanted to make sure Kayla would be okay with it too. They were a package deal.

He hadn't planned on asking her out today but the way she'd bitten her lip had short-circuited his brain and the invitation for drinks had popped out of his mouth before he could think better of it. And she'd said yes!

But he'd wait until after the party to bring it up again. He didn't want to make things weird, and then he'd be out yet another party entertainer.

Someone rang the doorbell, breaking into his thoughts.

Kayla's head popped up. "Is that Ms. Emma?"

Logan glanced at the microwave clock. "Should be. She said she'd come by early to set up the decorations."

Kayla abandoned her oatmeal and raced for the door.

"Remember to ask who it is first," Logan called as he followed her out of the kitchen.

"Who is it?" he heard Kayla shriek from beyond his view. He turned the corner just as Kayla pulled open the front door.

His pulse sped up at the sight of Emma beaming at Kayla. Emma radiated goodness and light, so bright she put the sun to shame. Was it any wonder he had it bad for her?

"Happy birthday, Kayla!" Emma was maneuvering a hand cart with three big plastic tubs on it, but when Kayla lunged forward to throw her arms around her waist, Emma released the cart and leaned down to wrap Kayla in a hug.

Logan stopped in the middle of the foyer, unable to take another step. The image they made stole his breath.

When Emma's gaze lifted and met his, he moved forward, as if drawn to her by an invisible force.

"Hi," she said, her voice soft.

"Hi." He swallowed hard and gestured at the cart. "Can I help you with that?"

"Yeah, will you take this to the backyard?" she asked, passing it to him. "I have a few more things to bring over."

"I'll go get them for you," he said.

"It's no trouble," she reassured him, then smiled down at Kayla, who still clung to her. "Do you want to help me, Kayla?"

Kayla slipped her hand into Emma's. "Can I, Daddy?"

"Sure, honey." Something twisted in his chest as he watched them go, Kayla chattering and Emma listening intently, their joined hands swinging as they walked. Kayla clearly felt comfortable around Emma, and with Lisette living so far away, Logan didn't want to jeopardize the growing bond between his daughter and a potential adult female role model. Maybe this vaguely-planned date was a mistake.

You're doing it again, he reminded himself while wrestling the unwieldy cart into the backyard. *Stop overthinking everything.*

He was unpacking the tubs when Kayla and Emma returned, each carrying a canvas tote bag. Kayla's said "Witch Please" and Emma's read "Boss Bruja." Logan snorted out a laugh.

As Kayla started digging through the bags and removing snacks for the party, Logan sidled up to Emma. "I was expecting the Birthday Witch." He gestured at her casual clothes. "You look just like my neighbor."

She sent him a flirty smirk and pointed at her chest. "Don't worry, I'm *100% that witch*, just like it says on my shirt."

He grinned. "Cute."

"I think you are, too," she said with a wink.

Before he could respond, Kayla bounded over with a question about the party games. Emma tried to assure them that she could set up on her own, but Kayla wanted to help, and Logan would have licked the ground if that's what Emma told him to do. Instead, she had them wrap a long folding table in black velvet and showed them how to twist green and purple crepe paper into chains. Logan had to admit, he was having fun, and he knew Kayla was too. He was amazed by the sheer number of witch hats and cauldrons in the décor, but once it was all done, the backyard looked pretty festive, and not—as he'd feared—like a Halloween explosion. Must have been the absence of pumpkins.

Emma went back home to change, but returned shortly to help Kayla dress and paint her face. Logan had put on a black t-shirt, and was surprised when Emma produced a black straw fedora for him, tricked out with cobwebs and a little gold skull.

"Dad has to participate too," Emma said as she reached up to settle the hat on his head. Kayla cackled with laughter when she saw him in it.

Emma was outfitted in a simple black dress with short sleeves, black shoes, and a wide-brimmed pointed hat made of sheer fabric embroidered with spiderwebs. She'd put on more makeup too—her eyes looked dark and mysterious, and her lips were painted a deep, velvety violet. Logan drank in the sight of her like it hadn't been thirty minutes since he'd last seen her.

Emma had brought a special dress for Kayla—black with a purple sash, green skirt, and gauzy black layers over the skirt. She painted glittery silver stars along Kayla's hairline and pinned a small purple witch's hat on Kayla's head. Logan had just finished pouring popcorn and potato chips into plastic cauldrons when the first guest arrived, ten minutes early. After that, it was chaos. Or at least, that was how it felt to him. Emma seemed perfectly unbothered, standing in the midst of a crowd of twelve screaming seven-and-eight-year-olds, leading them through "magic spells" and games, supervising the pizza and cupcake schedule, and making sure Kayla was the center of attention at all times. Meanwhile, Logan was kept busy handling the parents, who all wanted to talk to him about how to fast-track their third-graders for UCSD while he raced around doing things like grabbing extra napkins to mop up spilled "Goblin Green Juice" and finding stain remover when one of the kids dropped pizza on her mom's white shorts.

But he managed to take some photos and videos throughout the day, and in every single one, Kayla looked like she was having the time of her life.

The party was a success. And he had Emma to thank for that.

Once the last guest left and Kayla was sitting at the kitchen table starting on the Wonder Woman puzzle she'd been given as a gift, Logan helped Emma pack up.

"You were amazing," he said, dumping the dregs of pretzel sticks out of a cauldron.

She waved him off. "You're too kind."

"No, really. I don't know what I would have done if you hadn't come through today."

"It was my pleasure," she said, meeting his eyes across the table. "Kayla's a great kid, Logan."

"I know. I'm lucky."

She fell silent for a moment as she stacked unused plates and napkins with tiny ghosts on them. "I don't want to pry…"

"You can ask me anything," he told her. He'd known this was coming. She would ask about Lisette and—

"Have you never thrown a birthday party before?"

Logan blinked. That wasn't the question he'd been expecting. "Um, yes?"

"Was it…was it your first time doing it alone?"

Ah. There it was. "Kind of," he admitted. "Not because I'm divorced, though."

"Oh?" Her lips pressed together and she became rather focused on packing one of the big tubs, like she didn't want to ask more.

If they were going to do this, it was only fair that she know. "I've been divorced for about five years," he said. "Kayla's mom lives in Austin. It was amicable, but…we just had different visions for our lives."

"Logan, you don't have to—"

"No, it's okay. I want you to know." It had been ages since he'd talked to someone like this. About this. "I'm from the Bay Area, and my parents still live there. They helped a lot with Kayla, including all…this stuff." He gestured at the yard, strewn with spilled popcorn, crepe streamers, and balloons.

"I see," she said. And just when he started to worry that he'd pushed her away somehow, she sent him a small smile. "Well, I'm glad I was here to help you today."

"Me too," he murmured. She had no idea how glad he was. For a short time, he'd felt what it could be like to have a companion on this journey of parenthood. And he wanted it. Desperately.

He also just wanted Emma. With her expressive eyes and her coy smile, she stirred him up in a way he hadn't felt since…well, since too long.

Drinks. She'd agreed to have drinks with him, so they'd set a date for that and then see—

Kayla shouted for him from inside the house, and the moment

97

was broken before he could bring it up. Emma finished packing her party supplies and went home. And Logan was too tired to think about much else other than cleaning up. He'd text Emma tomorrow to ask when she wanted to get drinks.

He was in the kitchen tying up the trash when Kayla broached the topic.

"Daddy, I like Ms. Emma."

He paused with the garbage bag ties wrapped around his hands. Had she heard them talking? "You do?"

"Yeah. And I think you like her too."

Logan narrowed his eyes at his daughter's matter-of-fact tone. Kayla was still working on the puzzle, not even looking at him. "Why do you think that?"

"Because you always buy coffee on the days she works, even though you make it at home the other days."

Wow, was he that obvious? But Kayla wasn't done.

"And because some of the other moms try to talk to you, and you don't really talk to them, but you always make time to talk to Ms. Emma."

He raised an eyebrow at the inflection she put on "talk." *Flirt.* His daughter meant *flirt.* And she was right. A couple of the other moms tried to flirt with him occasionally, and while he didn't flirt back with them, he did, in fact, flirt with Emma whenever he got the chance.

"I wouldn't mind if Ms. Emma was your girlfriend," Kayla continued nonchalantly as she pressed a puzzle piece into the right spot.

Logan stifled a surprised laugh. He wouldn't mind either, but… "That's up to Ms. Emma, don't you think?"

Kayla shrugged. "I think she'd say yes, if you asked her." Then she shot him a pointed look that clearly said, *You should ask her, dummy.*

"We'll see," he said. Kayla rolled her eyes and returned her attention to the puzzle.

Logan finished tying the trash bag and took it outside to the bin. Before going back inside, he took a long look at Emma's bungalow. Apparently, he had his daughter's blessing to date the witch next door. Now what did he do with it?

CHAPTER THREE

AFTER CHANGING BACK into her "100% That Witch" t-shirt and a pair of denim shorts, Emma checked the time. She could still go to the park, if she wanted. The others would be there drumming and picnicking, and the bonfire wouldn't even get going until dusk.

But the fact was, she just didn't feel like it.

The holiday of Litha was all about the triumph of the light. Once, Emma's family had practiced the magic of their island. But after living in the northeast United States for four generations, they'd adopted the rituals that honored the change of seasons. As the first day of summer and the longest day, the Summer Solstice was a time to celebrate abundance—but also recognize the coming darkness as autumn grew closer and days became shorter.

How was she supposed to celebrate abundance when she felt like there was something big missing from her life?

Instead of going out, Emma brewed a cup of lemon tea and added honey from a local beekeeper who sold to the Witch's Brew Café. Taking her mug outside, she sat on the back porch steps. Clementine, her familiar, joined her.

"What should I do, Clem?" she asked the sleek black cat.

When Clem had shown up on Emma's first day in Bruja Cove, she'd looked to the sky and said, "Really? A black cat? Don't you all think that's a little cliché?" Clem had given Emma a sardonic look and headbutted her leg. They'd been inseparable ever since.

Now, Clem curled up by Emma's hip and nudged her hand.

Emma scratched the cat behind her velvety ears, and Clem purred.

"The party was fun, thanks for asking." Emma sipped her tea, then set it down on her other side. "But now that I've petted you, what do I do with the rest of the solstice?"

The sun was still high in the sky. A mile away was a park full of people who'd be happy to see her if she stopped by. And yet, Emma had never felt more alone.

She loved living in Bruja Cove. Loved her house and her work, both at the café and hosting parties for kids. Today, their enthusiasm had buoyed her spirits. Children lived each moment to the fullest, indulged in their emotions and wants without hiding them, stayed open to the intensity of life and all it had to offer. Every time she'd seen Kayla's happy smile, Emma had felt a surge of affection. There was magic in a child's smile, different from the magic Emma worked—or maybe not so much. It was all about the energy and emotion of the moment.

Not that Emma used magic at the parties. She didn't need to. All she needed to do was meet the children where they were, and make sure they felt seen and heard within her capacity as an entertainer. Wasn't that all anyone wanted, after all? To be seen and heard?

To be loved?

That was all Emma wanted now. Yes, she could appreciate the abundance in her life—a lovely home, wonderful friends, fulfilling work—but she wanted more. Wasn't it okay to want more? That wanting didn't mean she wasn't grateful for what she did have. But the more…it would be the icing on the cake. Just because she *could* be happy alone didn't mean she *had* to be alone.

Her thoughts turned to Logan. She liked him. Oh yeah, she *really* liked him. Somehow today was the first time she'd been inside his house, and she'd been impressed by how homey he'd made it in just a few months. There were paintings of ocean landscapes on the walls, unicorn-themed chapter books mixed with paperback thrillers on the coffee table, and a hand-crocheted blanket in blues and yellows spilled over the arm of the worn-in brown leather couch. The kitchen had smelled invitingly of cinnamon and coffee, reminding her of the café, making her wish she could just sit and chat. With both of them.

Because as much as she was attracted to Logan—and she lived for the moments when he dropped by the Brew—she was falling for Kayla as well. She was a sweet, thoughtful child, playful and smart, easy to be around. Just like her dad.

Emma sighed and took another sip of her tea. It was cooling, so she held the mug between both hands. Sucking in a breath through her nose, she exhaled sharply, channeling the burst of energy down her arms, through her palms, and into the tea. A faint wisp of steam rose from the lemon-scented water, and Emma sipped again. Perfect.

Annoyed at the interruption in petting, Clem bumped Emma's hip with her body, then turned and pushed something with her paw.

"What's that?" Emma asked, and let out a delighted laugh when the cat nudged an oak leaf toward her.

Emma picked it up by the stem and spun it between her fingers, watching as the light from the early evening sun filtered through the waxy green leaf, highlighting the yellow veins and the wavy edges.

"This is from my trip to the park a few days ago," Emma mused. "Clem, did you pull this out of the basket?"

Clem meowed and got to her feet. She flicked her tail and minced back into the house.

Emma picked up the mug and the leaf, then stood. The leaf had given her an idea—likely Clem's intention. Her familiar had a knack for providing clarity when Emma was feeling uncertain.

Inside, Emma picked up a woven basket full of oak leaves she'd foraged at the park and climbed the stairs to her attic workspace.

The upstairs space was what she thought of as her magic

room. It was where she did the majority of her spellcasting. Not because she wanted to keep it all hidden away—she had various magical paraphernalia scattered throughout the house—but because the lighting in here was magnificent. There were windows on both sides, facing the front and back of the little bungalow, plus a slanted skylight. She got sunlight all day long and stunning views of the moon at night. Under one window sat a long work table with potted plants along the back edge. Her altar was positioned beneath the opposite window. Bundles of dried herbs hung from the rafters, scenting the air with sage, lavender, and thyme. A low bookshelf held jars and books, and a small set of drawers was filled with candles, crystals, incense, tarot cards, and more.

Clem followed her in as she set the basket on the work table.

"You're right, Clem," Emma said. "I should put these leaves on the altar."

The black cat leaped onto the table and dropped something onto the surface. It was a round yellow flower with eight petals. Emma picked it up to examine it. It was a goldeneye, also known as a San Diego County sunflower. The bloom fit in the palm of her hand, the brilliant yellow making her think of the sun, which had reached its highest point in the sky just a few hours earlier.

"Thanks, Clem. Where'd you find this?"

Clem just turned her back and started cleaning her fur. She'd be busy for a while.

The light and shadows in the room shifted as Emma selected pieces for her Summer Solstice altar.

"Oak for strength and courage as we pass through the doorway into the second half of the year," she murmured, artfully arranging the leaves in the center of the table she used an altar.

"Goldeneye and yellow candles to symbolize the power of the sun." She placed Clem's blossom on top of the oak leaves and positioned six candles of different shapes and sizes in a semi-circle around the leaves.

Then she sprinkled dried chamomile flowers from a jar around the bases of the candles and over the oak leaves. "For luck," she whispered.

While she worked, Clem curled up in a ray of sunlight, yawned, and promptly fell asleep.

With the woodsy, herbaceous fragrance of chamomile clinging to her fingers, Emma sat on the round braided floor rug and opened the tiered wooden chest that housed her collection of crystals and rocks. As she sifted through the contents, which had been cleansed in the light of the full moon earlier that week, she debated how to proceed.

She could choose them by color. Yellow citrine for the sun, blue aquamarine—her birthstone—for the sky, green aventurine for the trees and grass. Or she could make her choices based on her intention for the next six months. But what did she want?

Be clear about what you desire, her horoscope had said. Time to get some clarity.

Closing her eyes, Emma took a few slow, deep breaths to center herself. She let the question simmer, and in the quiet of her heart, she had her answer. Opening her eyes, she went to the table and found a scrap of paper. After writing a single word on it, she stuck it in her pocket for later. Then she removed all the pink rose quartz from the box and settled the pieces on the altar between the candles.

"Rose quartz for—"

Before she could finish, her phone buzzed on the table with an incoming call, then let out a little jingle. Clem lifted her head and glared at it.

Glancing at the screen, Emma was surprised to see Logan's name flash. They'd emailed a few times about party details and payment, but this was the first time he'd called her.

Smiling, she accepted the call and held the phone to her ear. "Hey Logan, what's up?"

"*I need you.*"

Emma sucked in a breath at the raw desperation in his voice. Her skin flushed with heat. *Oh goddess,* she thought. *Finally.*

"Your help," Logan stammered. "I need your help. It's Kayla. She—"

"I'll be right over." Emma shoved the phone into her back pocket and bolted down the stairs.

CHAPTER FOUR

Logan met her at his front door. His thick, dark hair stood up in wild angles, and the corners of his mouth were pinched with stress.

"I'm sorry to bother—"

"It's no bother." Emma followed him inside. "What's going on? Where is she?"

"In her bedroom," he said, leading the way. "She was fine all evening—just working on her puzzle. But as I was getting her up to take a bath, she said she felt dizzy. She—she almost fainted, and she's running a fever. But I can't find the children's Tylenol. I know we brought some when we moved, but she hardly ever gets sick and I can't find it and I don't—"

"Logan." Emma gripped his arm to stop his rambling and force him to look at her. When he broke off, he was breathing hard, like he'd been running. She looked intently into his wild-eyed green gaze.

"Listen to me," she said. "I'm here now, okay? You're not alone."

The words seemed to cut through the haze of anxiety he was lost in. He nodded, a little too quickly. "Thanks. I'm sorry. You probably had your own plans, but—we don't really know too many people in town yet, and you're next door, and I trust you to stay with her while I run to the store and—"

"Hey." She gave his shoulder a little shake. "One thing at a time. Let me check on her."

"Yeah. Sure." He gestured to the open door at the end of the hall. "She's lying down."

Emma moved past him into Kayla's room. The room was dim, with only the desk light on, and the little girl was on her back in the bed. A wet washcloth covered her forehead, and she whimpered softly.

A small ottoman sat next to the bed. In the back of her mind, Emma imagined Logan perched there while he read Kayla bedtime stories. Now, Emma took the seat and carefully lifted the cold washcloth from Kayla's forehead. Kayla didn't even seem to notice she was there, which was worrisome.

Emma placed a hand on the child's forehead. The skin was clammy and hot, too hot, especially for having had a cold compress on it. Definitely a fever.

Twisting her body so Logan, who stood in the doorway, wouldn't see her, Emma sucked in a deep breath, then muttered a few words on the exhale. Her palm tingled as heat seeped into it, siphoning out of the child's body. Emma didn't take another breath until the little girl's brow smoothed and her breathing deepened. With a soft sigh, Emma took her hand away.

"It feels like her fever's abating," she said quietly, shifting back toward Logan.

He stood a few feet away, mouth agape, his eyes as wide as twin moons in his shocked face.

"What...what did you just do?" he stammered, his voice a hoarse rasp.

Ignoring the pounding in her chest, Emma pasted on an easy smile. "What do you mean?"

Logan pointed at Kayla. "I saw...it was like light moved from her head to your hand. You—" He strode forward and leaned over Emma to touch Kayla's cheek with the back of his hand. Then he gently pressed his palm to his daughter's forehead. His stunned gaze swung to Emma, then he caught her hand in his and stared at it.

Emma's breath caught in her throat as she stood, fear at his response mixing with tingles of desire from the stroke of his thumb over her heart line. "I only—" She stopped. She couldn't tell him what she was. But then his words caught up to her. "Hold on. You said you saw...light? On my hand?"

He dropped her hand and took a step back, rubbing the nape of his neck as if embarrassed. "Um, yeah."

He saw...

Emma gasped as everything clicked into place. Grabbing Logan's hand, she pulled him out of the room, leaving the door open so they could hear Kayla if she woke.

In the hallway, she kept her tone hushed, but excitement crept in. "Logan, you can see energy transfers. *I* can't even see those. What else can you see?" The question spilled out of her in a rush as all sorts of possibilities she'd never considered suddenly sprang to life. Her heart beat faster with the hope that maybe, just maybe...

"I can see some stuff," he admitted with a sheepish little shrug. "Stuff like...auras, and…" He gestured at his daughter, still sleeping peacefully. "Whatever you just did."

Well, this changed *everything*. Emma glanced at Kayla and asked softly, "Can she?"

"Yeah. Ever since she was a baby. They flock to her. I've heard her talking to them, but she won't give me details."

"Them?" Emma shot him a sharp look.

"Spirits," he said, like it was obvious. "Ghosts."

Emma's eyebrows rose. "Can you see them too?"

He hesitated, then nodded. "Just glimmers. They don't interact with me as much as they do with her."

Bright, brilliant joy welled up in Emma's chest. "Logan," she said. "I'm a witch."

"I know," he said.

"No, I mean, like a *real* witch. Not just for parties."

He gave her t-shirt a pointed glance. "Yeah, I'd pretty much figured that out."

"And you're okay with that?" She had to be sure.

He gave her an exasperated look. "Emma, I just told you I see ghosts. And you saved my daughter. How could I not be okay with it?"

She waved him off. "I didn't *save* her. She was out in the sun too long. Some rest, water, and a children's Tylenol would have cleared it right up. I just sped up the process."

His voice dropped then, and that familiar heat was back in his eyes. "It might seem like nothing to you, but I think you're amazing."

With the danger past and the truth out in the open, the air between them became charged with something hot and electric.

Suddenly, it no longer seemed like such a bad idea to get involved with the single dad next door.

Just then, Kayla rolled over and burrowed into her pillow. "Close the door," she mumbled grumpily. "I'm trying to sleep here."

"Sorry," they whispered in unison. Emma smothered a laugh while Logan eased the bedroom door shut.

In the relative privacy of the hallway, his eyes met hers again.

"Do you want to sit on the back porch?" he asked. "Have that drink?"

Emma swallowed. This was it. No going back.

"Yes. Let's."

She followed him down the hall to the kitchen, were a bottle of wine sat breathing on the counter, next to two glasses.

"Expecting someone?" She raised an eyebrow at the glasses.

"I was thinking of texting you," he replied ruefully. "Before Kayla's fever, that is."

"Well, here I am." With a smile, Emma opened the back door to let him through, then shut it quietly behind them. The sun was setting, lighting up the sky in vibrant orange and pink hues, gilding everything in a soft, warm glow. They sat on the porch swing, rocking softly. Logan filled their glasses with a fruity, fragrant Shiraz, then set the open bottle on a small table beside the swing.

"Cheers," he said, his voice hushed, as if reluctant to disturb the sunset stillness surrounding them. "Happy summer solstice."

"Blessed Litha," Emma replied, and with their gazes locked, they clinked their glasses together.

Emma took a sip, enjoying the burst of ripe, fruity berry flavors in her mouth. The wine made her think of the same flavors sliding over *his* tongue, which made her think of *her* tongue sliding over *his* tongue, and then—

"How do you typically celebrate Litha?" Logan asked, and Emma cleared her throat.

"At night? With a bonfire."

"Oh yeah?" His dark eyebrow quirked. "Well, we have a fire pit."

The warmth that spread through her chest wasn't desire, although she still felt that. This was...oof. *Feelings.* She was catching some real feelings for this guy. He wasn't just the cute neighbor she sometimes sold coffee to. She felt comfortable with him, like it was the easiest thing in the world to be by his side.

For a woman with a big witchy secret, this sense of ease was a rare sensation.

"I'd love to," she said softly.

He took her hand again and led her to the back of the yard where a brick patio held a round metal fire pit, ringed by four Adirondack chairs. Emma sipped her wine and waited while he pulled wood from beneath a tarp and set it up in the fire pit. But when he reached for the firestarter kit, she put a hand on his shoulder to stop him.

"I got this," she said.

His eyebrows jumped up and a delighted smile lit his handsome face.

After setting down her wine, Emma stepped forward toward the fire pit, anticipation zinging through her. What a blessing to be able to show him the entirety of herself! She raised both hands and held them palm out toward the expertly built cone of logs.

Deep breath, slow exhale. The familiar energy spiraled down her arms, out her hands, and—

The logs burst into flame.

Logan let out a low whistle. "I'm impressed."

"I'm an elemental witch," she explained. "Pretty good at doing stuff with fire, if I do say so myself."

His lips curved and he dropped his voice into a mock-sexy drawl. "Is that why you're so hot?"

Emma snorted out a laugh and he cringed.

"Sorry. These days I'm better versed in dad jokes than flirting."

Emma reached for his hand and gently pulled him toward her. "Don't apologize. I like how you flirt with me."

At her touch, the lines of his face softened, a stark contrast to how he'd looked when she'd arrived. The fire reflected in his sea glass-green eyes. Or maybe it was the reflection of her own desire. "I was wondering if you'd noticed."

The revelation of her secret—and his—made her bold. What did she have to lose? She swayed toward him. "And I'm wondering if you're ever going to kiss me."

The burning embers she'd seen in his gaze for months finally ignited into an inferno. He cupped the back of her head and before she could take a breath, his mouth was on hers.

Heat exploded through her, a thousand tiny detonations along all of her nerve endings. She stretched her arms around his neck, clinging to him as his lips moved over hers. She opened, allowing him in, tasting the wine on his tongue as she'd imagined just a few minutes earlier.

The reality was a thousand times better than she'd envisioned. It was electric and vivid and *true*.

With the fire crackling beside them and the setting sun at her back, Emma lost herself in his kiss, in the slide of his tongue, in the feel of his arm wrapped tight and strong around her waist, in the press of their bodies together.

They broke the kiss, both gasping. Logan pressed his forehead to hers.

"I meant to talk more before trying to kiss you," he confessed.

She leaned in and nipped at his lower lip. "I'm sorry. I got tired of waiting."

Chuckling, he stroked a hand down the side of her face, gently pushing the loose strands of hair that had escaped from her braid behind her ear. His gaze captured hers, as it had from the first day she'd seen him walk into the Witch's Brew.

"I really like you, Emma," he said quietly.

The warmth of his words seeped into her bones and settled like a soothing hearth fire. "I like you too, Logan."

"You know, Kayla said she wouldn't mind if you were my girlfriend."

Emma smothered a laugh. "Did she really?"

"Sure did. So, we have her blessing."

"That's good to know." A quiet sense of joy spread through her. "Maybe we should listen to her. She's pretty smart."

"I know. But too observant for her own good. She pointed out that I always buy coffee when you're at the café, even though I know how to make it at home."

Emma bit her lip to keep from smiling. "I noticed that, too."

He shifted, looking down at her tucked into the curve of his arm. His expression was serious now, earnest. "Could we maybe, I don't know, try a real date sometime?"

"This isn't a real date?" she teased.

He glanced down at their wine glasses, at the fire, at the darkening sky. A slow smile curved his lips. "You're right. This is a perfect date."

"I couldn't have dreamed of better." Then she reached into her pocket and pulled out the folded slip of paper. Holding it between her fingertips, she sent a little flare of energy into it. It ignited with a tiny hiss, and she leaned forward to toss it into the fire pit. It joined the larger inferno and quickly curled and crumbled into ash. The particles drifted upward into the sky, borne by the winds of the crackling flames. Emma felt it float away and disperse, her wish traveling out into the greater universe, connected to her by a thread of energy, of intention.

"What was that?" Logan asked, once she'd slipped her arm back around his waist.

She snuggled against him, breathing in the scents of fire, of trees, of man. Scents of summer, and beyond. "A dream come true," she whispered, tilting her face upward for his kiss. "Just like you."

COMING SOON FROM ALEXIS DARIA

From Alexis Daria, author of the critically acclaimed, international bestseller *You Had Me at Hola*, comes a fun, sexy romance set against a reality dance show.

Gina Morales wants to make it big. But in her four seasons on *The Dance Off*, she's never even made it to the finals—though her latest partner, the sexy star of an Alaskan wilderness show, could be her chance. Who knew the strong, silent, survivalist-type had moves like that? She thinks Stone Nielson is her ticket to win it all. That is until her producer makes it clear they're being set up for a showmance.

Joining a celebrity dance competition is the last thing Stone wants. However, he'll endure anything to help his family, even as he fears revealing their secrets. While the fast pace of Los Angeles makes him long for the peace and privacy of home, he can't hide his growing attraction for his dance partner. Neither wants to fake a romance for the cameras, but the explosive chemistry that flares between them is undeniable.

As Stone and Gina heat up the dance floor, the tabloids catch on to their developing romance. With the spotlight threatening to ruin everything, will they choose fame and fortune or let love take the lead?

☾

Along Came Amor
Copyright © 2023 by Alexis Daria
Available 2023 from Avon Books

From international bestselling author Alexis Daria comes the final installment in the critically acclaimed Primas of Power series, where a divorced middle school teacher discovers that her perfect no-strings fling is anything but.

No strings

After Ava Rodriguez's now-ex-husband declares he wants to "follow his dreams"—which no longer include her—she's left questioning everything she thought she wanted. So when a handsome hotelier flirts with her soon after her divorce is finalized, Ava vows to stop overthinking and embrace the opportunity for an epic one-night-stand.

No feelings

Roman Vasquez's sole focus is the empire he built from the ground up. He lives and dies by his schedule, but the gorgeous stranger grimacing into her cocktail glass inspires him to change his plans for the evening. At first, it's easy for Roman to agree to Ava's rules. But one night isn't enough, and the more they meet, the more he wants.

No falling in love

Roman is the perfect fling, until Ava sees him at her cousin's engagement party—as the groom's best man, no less! Suddenly, maintaining her boundaries becomes a lot more complicated as she tries to hide the truth of their relationship from her family. However, Roman isn't content being her dirty little secret, and he doesn't just want more, he wants everything. With her future uncertain and her family pressuring her from all sides, Ava will have to decide if love is worth the risk—again.

ABOUT THE AUTHOR

Alexis Daria is an award-winning and bestselling romance author. Her debut novel, *Take the Lead*, was a RITA Award winner for Best First Book, and *You Had Me at Hola*, the first in her Primas of Power series, is an international bestseller. Alexis's books have been featured on several "Best of" lists from outlets like *Oprah Magazine*, *Entertainment Weekly*, *NPR*, *Buzzfeed*, and the *Washington Post*, and have received starred reviews from trade publications like *Publishers Weekly*, *Kirkus*, and *Library Journal*. A former visual artist, Alexis is a lifelong New Yorker who loves Broadway musicals and pizza.

For updates and exclusive content, follow Alexis's newsletter: alexisdaria.com/newsletter/.

You can also catch up with Alexis on Instagram: @alexisdaria.

Made in United States
North Haven, CT
10 February 2023

32363091R00075